THE PURSUIT OF...

A WORTH SAGA PRELUDE

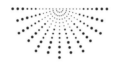

COURTNEY MILAN

For everyone who waited to be included in the sequel—and particularly for those who are still waiting.

CHAPTER ONE

Yorktown, 1781

I n the heat of battle, Corporal John Hunter could never differentiate between silence and absolute noise. Years had passed since his first engagement, but every time, the sheer discord of sound blended together. The cry of bugles sounding orders, the clash of bayonets, the rat-tat-tat of firearms somewhere in the distance, the hollow concussion of the cannons—each one of those things heralded someone's doom. To take heed to any of it was to fall into fear. To fear was to make mistakes; to err was to die. No matter the odds, the sounds of battle were so overwhelming that they were no different than silence.

Yorktown was just like any other engagement.

Oh, the strategists might have begged to differ. There were more clouds, more night. Less frost than some of the battles he'd taken part in. Someone had talked prettily at them about how the freedom of this nascent nation was at stake and some other things John had listened to with his hands curling into fists. The colonies didn't care about John's freedom, so he returned the favor by not caring about theirs.

In the end, all battles were smoke and shit and death, and John's only goal was to see the other side of this war without being forcibly acquainted with the Grim Reaper. Fight. Survive. Go home to his family. The most basic of needs.

The night was dark around him and his fellow infantrymen. The spiked branches of the abatis had left scratches on his arm; the charge up the scarp had John's heart pounding.

They'd crept through the ditch and were approaching the final defenses of Redoubt Ten—a wall of sharp stakes, somewhat battered. A group of fools ahead of him was negotiating how best to storm the parapet. John held back. Apparently, the idiot in command of this maneuver wanted to lead the charge. Sutton, one of the other black men assigned to storm the redoubt, was hoisting him up.

Nothing to do but join them and hope for the best. Nothing to do but survive, fight, and return to his family before anything ill happened to them. Fight, survive—

John stilled, the chant in his head dying down.

There was a reason he let the background noise of battle fade to nothingness in his mind. It left room for wariness and suspicion. There. Behind them, back toward the abatis— there was a shadow.

It moved, man-shaped.

The person behind them was large and almost invisible, and he lay in wait. John's comrades hadn't noticed him. In their haste to get in, they'd all left themselves vulnerable.

All of them but him.

Damn it all to hell.

Silence and noise mingled in John's head. Perhaps the gunfire from the feint on Fusiliers Redoubt a ways off was loud; perhaps it was nothing. Perhaps the man he saw screamed in defiance as John turned toward him; perhaps he was silent.

Fight. Survive... *Damn* it.

There was no hope for it. John couldn't wait to see what would happen. He lowered his weapon, said a prayer for his sister, should his soul become irreparably detached from his body, and sprinted back toward the shadowed branches of the abatis.

The man's head tilted. John braced himself, waiting for the man to fire a weapon or raise a blade, but instead the fellow just waited in silence. One second. Two.

John crashed into him at full speed, driving his shoulder into the man's chest. God, the other man was huge. The impact traveled bruisingly through his body. Still, John wasn't exactly tiny himself. They fell together, hitting the ground. It took one moment to get his bayonet into position, another to drive it forward, blade seeking the other man's belly.

It didn't make contact. Instead, the fellow hit John on the head with the butt of his musket. John's head rang; he shook it, pushed the echoing pain aside, and rolled out of the way of the next bayonet strike.

There was no time to think, no time to come up with any plan except to survive the next instant, then the next. No room for fine blade work, either; John swung his musket like a staff.

The other man blocked the strike, and the force of gun barrel meeting gun barrel traveled up John's arm. The battle had all but disappeared into a pinprick, into this moment between two men.

"God," the other fellow said. "You're strong."

John refused to hear his words.

John had neither energy nor emotion to waste on conversation. Fight. Survive the war. Go back to Lizzie and Noah and his mother. He'd *promised* them he would—stupid promise, that—but he'd break the entire British Army before he broke that promise. Men who let their attention slip perished, and he had no intention of perishing. He gritted his teeth and tried to smash the other man's head.

The other man ducked out of the way. "Nice weather for a siege, isn't it?"

John's almost perfect concentration slipped. What the devil was that supposed to mean? Nice weather for a *siege?* Did that mean the weather was good—it wasn't—or that bad weather was preferable during a siege? And what did *preferable* even mean between the two of them? Siegers and the besieged had different preferences.

Ah, damn it.

This was why John couldn't let himself listen to battle. Anything—everything—could be a distraction. He shook his head instead and threw his entire weight behind his next strike.

It wasn't enough; the other man was taller and heavier, and their bayonets crossed once more. He was close enough to see features—stubble on cheeks, sharp nose, the glint of some distant bombardment reflected in the man's eyes. They held their places for a moment, shoulders braced together, their heaving breaths temporarily synchronized.

"It's your turn," the man said with an unholy degree of cheer. "I remarked on the weather. Etiquette demands that you say something in return."

For a moment, John stared at the fellow in utter confusion. "I'm bloody trying to kill you. This is a battle, not a ball."

He pivoted on one foot, putting his entire back into whirling his weapon. This time he managed to whack the other man's stomach. A blow—not a hard one, he hadn't the space to gather momentum—but enough that the fellow grunted and staggered back a pace.

"Yes," the man said, recovering his balance all too quickly, "true, completely true, we *are* trying to commit murder upon each other. That doesn't mean that we need to be impolite about it."

Fucking British. Would he call a halt to take tea, too?

"If you prefer," the man continued, sidestepping another blow, "you could try, 'Die, imperialist scum.' The moniker is somewhat lacking in friendly appeal, but it has the benefit of being true. I own it; we are imperialist scum."

What the *hell?*

"But aren't we both?" The conversation, like the battle, seemed interminable. "You colonials are displacing natives as well. I will give you this point. You'd be quite right not to use that particular insult. It would be rather hypocritical."

Not for John, it wouldn't. His presence in this land could not be put down to any volition on the part of his black mother, who was the only ancestor the colonials counted. But now was not a time for the fine nuances of that particular discussion. It was not, in fact, the time for any discussion at all.

He swung his musket again, heard the crack of the weapon against the barrel of the other man's musket.

"It just goes to show. Politics is obviously not a good choice of conversation among strangers, I suppose. My father always did say that, and damn his soul, he is occasionally right. What of books? Have you read anything recently?"

There were still a few soldiers making their way through the abatis, streaming past them. One went by now, glancing in their direction.

"Can't we try to kill each other in silence?" John snuck out a foot, attempting to trip the other man. His enemy danced away.

"Ah, is that it?" The man brightened. "I see. You can't fight and talk at the same time? My friend, Lieutenant Radley, was exactly the same way. I drove him mad, he used to say."

Used to? Ha. As if anyone could ever become accustomed to this jibber-jabber.

"He died in battle," the other man continued, "so possibly he was right. You probably shouldn't listen to my advice on this score. I don't have the best record."

Their weapons crossed again.

"Except"—unbelievably, he was still talking—"I obviously should not have told you that. I've given away an important advantage. Damn it. My father was right again. 'Think before you speak,' he always used to say. I *hate* when my father is right."

John didn't want to think of this man as someone with family, with friends. War was hell enough when you were just killing nameless, faceless individuals.

There was nothing to do but get it over with as quickly as possible, before he started thinking of his enemy as a person.

He threw himself forward, caught the other man's shoulder with his, and managed to send him off balance. A moment, just a moment; enough for John to clip his hand smartly with the butt of his musket. The weapon the man had been holding went flying. John hooked one foot around the man's ankle; his opponent landed flat on his back. John pushed the tip of his blade into the man's throat.

The man's hands immediately shot above his head. "I surrender the redoubt!"

John froze in place. "Have you the authority to do that?"

"No," the other man answered, "but let's be honest, it's only a matter of time, don't you think? Excellent tactics on your part. I almost didn't see you coming. Somebody ought to surrender it eventually. Why not me?"

"Sorry," John said, and it was quite possibly the first time he'd ever apologized to an enemy on the battlefield. "I'm going to have to kill you."

"Ah, well," the other man said. "You know your duty. Be quick about it, if you must. Better me than you, don't you think?"

Literally no other person had ever said that to John on the battlefield. John frowned down at the man in front of him, and…

And, oh Christ. He suddenly realized that he'd heard of this man. His friend Marcelo had mentioned something about encountering him before. British officer. Tall. Meaty. Blond. He'd chalked the tale up to campfire boasting. When he'd heard there was a madman who couldn't stop talking, John had imagined something along the lines of a berserker, frothing at the mouth. He hadn't expected a mere prattle-basket.

"*I* think it's better me than you," John said, frowning down at the man. "You can't possibly agree."

A flare from the battle reflected in the other man's eyes, temporarily illuminating him. John didn't want to see his face. He didn't want to see the haunted expression in his eyes. He didn't want to remember him as a person. He should never have let the clamor of battle give way to the sound of conversation, because he suspected that the tone of this man's voice—all gravel and regret—would stay with him all the rest of his days.

"Don't make me go back," the man said, so at odds with his cheery conversation on politics. "I can't go back to England. Dying is not my preferred form of non-return, but for the past months it's the only one I've been able to think of."

John tightened his grip on the musket. He couldn't listen. He couldn't think. In battle, he could only allow himself to be a husk, an automaton. Fight. Survive. Killing was a necessary part of war. He'd learned not to look too hard at his enemies, not to ask too many questions. He'd learned not to let himself dwell too much on the men who perished at the other end of his musket.

It was always a mistake to listen during battle. Here he was, hesitating, when it was either John or the man who'd asked him about books and the weather. He could make it painless—as painless as death by bayonet ever was.

The man gave him a sad smile. "It's nice weather for dying, isn't it?"

He was lying. He had to be lying. This was the sort of thing for a lying officer to do—to converse politely, as if manners meant a damned thing on the battlefield. John pushed his bayonet down a quarter inch.

"Go on," the man said.

His permission made it even harder. John didn't want to do it, but it was John or the prattle-basket, John or the prattle-basket, and John had come too far to perish now.

A bugle sounded.

John looked up into chaos. He could hear cheers, could see the lieutenant colonel in charge of this attack—Hamilton, was it not?—clapping one of the soldiers on the back. Ah, the idiot in command had survived storming the parapet after all. While John had been fighting, his fellow soldiers had stormed the redoubt and taken it.

It was done. They'd won.

He eased up on the bayonet. "It's your lucky day. You're a prisoner now, instead of a dead man."

"No." The man's hand clasped around the musket barrel, holding the bayonet in place. "No. You have to do it."

"What?" John stared at him.

"You have to do it," the man instructed. "Do you understand? If you Americans take the redoubt, Yorktown falls. If

Yorktown falls, the war is over. If you don't kill me now, they'll make me go back to Britain, and I *can't* go back."

"Can't?" John swallowed and looked down.

"Can't." The man shut his eyes.

They'd called him a madman, and John had imagined a demon on the battlefield, not a man who talked of politics.

Perhaps it was mad to prefer death to a return to a place that could never be called home, but if that was madness, it was a madness John knew. He'd once been enslaved. He knew what it was like to yearn for freedom, to prefer death to a return to a state that robbed him of choice, of freedom, of humanity. The fellow was obviously given to dramatics. John doubted anything so horrid waited for him back in England. Still... He understood.

He didn't want to have anything in common with a blond British officer...but he did.

He should take the man prisoner. Should call for rein-forcements. Who knew what this man would do if John gave him the opportunity?

"I can't go back," the man said again.

John should never have listened. Damn it, damn it, damn it. He swore and threw down his weapon.

The man struggled, propping himself up on his elbows.

"Then don't." John took off his coat. "Here." He held the garment out.

It wasn't much—a bit tattered, and God knew what it smelled like; John couldn't detect the stench any longer.

The man stared at it.

"It's not red." John shook the coat. "It's a mess out there as it is. Get muddy enough and nobody will know who you are. If you don't want to go back to Britain, turn into an Ameri-can. You talk enough; I'm sure you can come up with a believable lie. Get out of here. Don't go back."

The man stared at him. "Why would you let me go? I'm the enemy."

"Enemy?" John rolled his eyes. "Take a good look at me. I have little love for...what did you call them? The colonial brand of imperialist scum. I have no enemies, just people I fight on a battlefield."

The officer sat up. Looked at John. John knew what he was seeing—not the broad shoulders, not the determination John knew flashed in his own eyes, nor the set of his square jaw. No, this blond prattler who talked of manners and politics would see only the brown of his skin.

John was an idiot to offer anything. But he knew too well what it was like to have no hope of help and to find it anyway.

Here, he thought to the woman at the well who had shaken her head, denying his existence to the man who sought John. John had crouched hidden behind the bushes until the threat had passed. She'd looked at him then. She hadn't spoken; she'd only nodded and left, as if she hadn't changed his life with that simple denial. *Here. I'm paying you back for that after all.*

"I don't want to talk to you," John said. "I don't want to be your friend. I'll kill you on the battlefield if I have to. But if you're desperate enough to die, you're desperate enough to abscond. If you don't want to go back, get rid of your damned officer's coat and take mine."

The man stared up at him. He looked at the coat, at the musket that John had tossed aside.

Slowly, he took John's coat. "I won't forget this," he said. "I'll pay you back someday."

John had heard that particular promise before. He'd heard it when he saved his father from being crushed by a falling mast. He'd heard it when he'd rescued another man in the Rhode Island First on the battlefield. Half the time, white men didn't even bother with empty words to assuage their consciences—at least not to the likes of him. The other half? They never remembered their promises. They didn't have to.

John shook his head. "Don't bother."

"John?" Elijah's call came from further in. "John, is that you down there? Are you wounded?"

He turned, leaving the British officer alone with his coat. He was already faintly regretting his choice—the late-autumn night was cold enough that he'd want that coat before morning struck.

He would never see the man again.

In the dark of the night, the man had no idea what John even looked like. Even if it were day, he'd never be able to distinguish John from any other black man. White men rarely could.

"I'm Henry," the officer called after him. "Henry Latham, at your service."

Henry Latham no doubt thought he was an honorable fellow. He'd tell himself that one day he'd return the favor, just as he assiduously avoided contact with anyone who looked like John. There was little use puncturing his illusions.

John knew that the roll of his eyes was hidden by the night, so he took care to imbue an extra dose of sarcasm in his tone. "I'll be sure to remember that."

"John?" Elijah was coming closer. "John, are you well?"

"I'm alive," John called in return. "Alive and unharmed." His body was already protesting the *unharmed* designation, his shoulder twingeing, his head still hurting.

Ha. He had already forgotten the name. He'd never hear from the man again.

❧

Some days later...

Henry Latham knew that time was running out.

Well. Not in the literal sense. Time never ran out. It only ran on, continuing at its own inevitable pace. But in a little while the Continental Army would be on the move again, following the inevitable peace accords. The time it would take him to find John would be massively increased once that happened.

In addition, there was the problem of Henry himself. Some men prided themselves on remembering and repaying every obligation. Henry...well. He always *intended* to pay his debts, but then...he forgot. He could never keep any one thing at the forefront of his mind long enough to concentrate on it. This time, though, it would be different. This was New Henry, and New Henry was...

New Henry was confused, baffled, and on the run from the British Army. That made him exactly like Old Henry, except he'd overtly committed treason and absconded in the heat of battle.

Technically, it had been after the redoubt was surrendered, but not by much. If that wasn't the heat of battle, it was perhaps the warmth of it.

The good thing about war was that it had proven all too easy to sell a few items of personal jewelry for funds—so many others were fleeing—without drawing much attention. New Henry had money. New Henry had clothing. New Henry just needed a plan. His started like this:

1. Find John. By his uniform, he was a corporal, most likely in the Rhode Island Regiment, although Henry had not been able to verify that for certain. Family name? Hometown? All unknown, but that was no reason to discard a perfectly good first step, especially when the remainder of his plan looked like this.

2. …?

3. …!?

4. …

5. Cheese? Maybe cheese. Cheese was good.

Taking John's jacket and running off had been undoubtedly the most impulsive decision he had ever made in a life predicated upon what his father called rash whim and unpremeditated fancy.

As it was, he had a name—John—and a face and a rank. He'd made inquiries—not careful ones; nothing Henry did could ever truly be called careful—and found that there *had* been black soldiers under the First Rhode Island Regiment, and as the Rhode Island forces had been decimated, the resulting Rhode Island Regiment been pulled piecemeal into the assault on Yorktown. It was a start.

John, maybe from Rhode Island. He *could* wait years and lose all hope of the trail, or he could do what he was doing now: He could walk up to the enemy encampment with nothing more than a smile and a pack containing his secret weapon.

He sauntered up to the soldiers standing guard at the entrance to the camp and smiled as if he belonged.

"A good day to you, gentlemen."

They exchanged suspicious glances.

Ah, damn. The accent. Henry's accent marked him as a creature of exclusive British public schools and that terrible year at Oxford before everyone—from his father to the dean to the unfortunate brace of goats that he really hadn't meant to send down the Cherwell on a barge—agreed that further schooling was probably not in anybody's best interests.

But Americans came from Britain, too.

The two soldiers frowned at him.

Henry just smiled at them. "If I could impose on you for some assistance, I would be deeply in your debt."

The men continued to stare at him without blinking. How they managed to do that, Henry would never know. It was a useful skill, not blinking. Did their eyes not dry? How did they accomplish that?

Oh. No. The one on the right blinked. Ah, well. So much for that theory.

"I am a cheesemonger," Henry said. It was a complete lie, but the story almost didn't matter. "Cheese is my livelihood. I am here for the purpose of purveying cheese."

The men exchanged confused glances and Henry made a mental note: Next time, less emphasis on cheese.

"We don't want any cheese," one finally said. "Move along."

"Oh, ha! I'm not here to mong my cheese at you."

Blank stares met this.

Was *mong* even a verb? It had to be; what else did a monger do, if not mong?

"I encountered a soldier of your company in town," Henry said. "He coveted my cheese—my delicious, crumbly, fragrant cheese." Emphasis on *fragrant*. Henry had smelled infantrymen five months from a bath who reeked less than the cheese wrapped in his pack. "He wanted a bit for his journey home and asked me to bring a goodly amount by."

The two men softened incrementally.

"I'd hoped you might be able to direct me in his...ah, direction."

"Who is it?"

"John," Henry said brightly. "He's a corporal!"

"John. *Which* John? What regiment?"

"Ah... I've forgotten his family name."

Oh, *that* made the story *so* believable. Who introduced themselves as only John? What a mess.

Henry went on brightly. "He's an inch or so taller than I am. Muscular." Henry still had bruises. "Deep voice. In the

Rhode Island Regiment, I believe. He's one of the Negro soldiers."

Their faces changed on that last word, closing even more than they'd already closed before.

"One of the Black Regiment, then." The one on the right gestured. "They're over there. *We* wouldn't know any of them by name."

Henry thanked them and left.

He wondered, briefly, how they managed the headaches that must plague them with that attitude. He'd struggled with his own confusion for long enough before coming to his not-so-ideal strategy, but then, he was no great intellect.

He'd thought maybe in the infantry, it would be different. After all, these men were fighting for their ideals. It wouldn't, he'd told himself, be like the British Army, with its rules and regulations and safeguards.

It seemed exactly like the British Army, down to the sneers. Maybe sewing stars and stripes atop a flawed fabric didn't change the cloth. But there he went again. He was going to give himself a headache trying to puzzle it out. Henry shook his head and made his way in the direction the two men had indicated.

"I'm looking for John," he said, when he'd found the encampment of black soldiers. "This tall"—he gestured— "strong, taciturn, participated in the assault on Redoubt Ten, from...the Rhode Island Regiment?"

A fellow stood. "What do you want with John?"

"I'm a cheesemonger." Henry considered the rest of his speech. "He asked to buy some of my cheese."

The man looked at one of his fellows. "Huh," said the one who was sitting, examining boots that were as much hole as leather. "Cheese. I hadn't thought..."

"It's very excellent cheese," Henry assured him. "And I promised him a discount."

"What can it hurt?" one of them said. "Hunter is heading out. It's not impossible. I'll take you to him."

Hunter. Hunter. He was John Hunter. Excellent.

"Cheese," one of them muttered.

They conducted Henry through the darkening camp to a fire at the edge where a few men sat.

"John, this man—"

John looked up. In the days since the assault, Henry had tried to remember what his... benefactor? enemy? looked like. Tall, he remembered. He could have drawn the line of the other man's profile, the prominent, chiseled ridges of the eyebrows, the shape of his nose.

This was the first time Henry had seen him in daylight, fading though it was. John, last name previously unknown, learned and...drat it, immediately forgotten again. Their eyes met, and Henry felt a current sweep through him. *Him*, Henry thought, one hand going to his heart. *Him.*

This man. There was a scar down his cheek—not prominent, just a line of darker brown slashed across his face. His eyes narrowed.

They'd talked that night—well, to be fair, *Henry* had talked. Still, fucking was the only thing more intimate than fighting. He'd seen *something* even in the darkness. In daylight it was more obvious.

John was utterly, bewitchingly lovely, and Henry had been already predisposed to bewitchment. His cheekbones were high. He wasn't as tall as Henry remembered—something about a man trying to kill you made him loom in the imagination—but he was well muscled. John's arm was bound with some kind of cloth in a sling, holding it against his chest. His lips pressed into a thin line as he looked at Henry.

Something deep in Henry's gut awoke in that moment. It felt like a fundamental shift in his makeup. It was like the circular all over again. He changed again now, his breath cycling through him. He would never be the same.

Henry forgot everything he was going to say.

"John," the man beside him said. "This fellow says you're buying his cheese."

"Cheese?" John frowned. "I didn't want any cheese."

"Cheese?" Henry said, momentarily forgetting his own story. "What cheese?"

The man who had brought him looked at him. "What do you mean, 'what cheese'?"

"Oh. *Cheese*. Right. Never mind the cheese. John, it's Henry Latham." There were various other titles and whatnot that people often insisted on adding to his name, but they were all embarrassing and irrelevant in the moment.

John wrinkled his nose in confusion. "Who? I don't know a Henry Latham. What do you have to do with cheese?"

"The cheese is a lie," Henry explained brightly.

"What the hell?" the man muttered behind him. "I *knew* something was amiss. Wait. I recognize him. John, this man is a British officer. I've fought him before. I told you about him."

John looked up. His eyes narrowed, and he looked at Henry in something like astonishment.

"Nonsense," Henry said brightly. "If I were a British officer, I certainly wouldn't be waltzing around over here out of uniform, would I?"

John stared at him.

"You remember me, don't you? We met outside Yorktown. We talked about imperialism?"

"My God," John said slowly.

"You actually know him?" That was from the man in the back. "Are you sure he's not a British officer?"

"I do." John swallowed. "I suppose that if he says he's not a

British officer, he's not a British officer. How curious, though. He's shorter than I remember."

Henry couldn't help but smile. "I knew you'd not have forgotten! And how could you doubt me? I told you I would find you, didn't I? And here I am."

John just looked at him. He did not look delighted. He looked surprised and suspicious. "Here you are," he repeated. "What the devil are you doing here?"

CHAPTER TWO

John had not thought of that bizarre conflict since the battle. There had been no point. The entire encounter felt like a dream, possibly a nightmare. The scene from his memory was tinged with the dark blue of midnight, with a sense of confused detachment from reality.

Did that really happen? He wasn't even sure, now, with the man standing directly in front of him.

But the man was here and he had a name. In daylight, he made less sense than he had at night. He was tall—but not, as John seemed to remember, *taller*. His hair was not blond; it stood up in little tufts that were not quite orange, not quite yellow. His eyes darted about with a sense of curiosity reflected in the nervous energy he radiated.

"Why the devil are you here?" It made no sense, and John didn't trust things that made no sense.

"I told you I'd search you out."

"Neither of us believed that."

"Speak for yourself." Latham gave him a brilliant smile. "I owe you my life. *You* may think that's a debt of little value; *I* have another view on it."

"He's not selling cheese?" Elijah, standing behind Latham, frowned. "John, do you want us to…?"

"He's harmless." At least, he was unlikely to do harm at this point. John would shake his hand, or whatever the man expected, and see the last of him. In fact, there was one sure way to drive the man off—invite him to sit with the black soldiers. "Here," John said with a casual solicitousness. "Sit down. Share a campfire. Stay for supper. What was your name again?"

"Latham." The man set his pack down and sat cross-legged on the ground. "Henry Latham. Can I offer anything for the common pot?"

Behind him, Elijah shrugged in confusion. And no surprise—even the most committed abolitionists often balked at sharing food with black soldiers. Then again, Latham had already proven himself to be more than a bit unusual.

He was rummaging in his pack. "I've a bit of bread and butter, if that wouldn't go amiss, and rather a lot of cheese. I don't recommend the cheese. It's a decoy."

"What is decoy cheese?" Marcelo had enlisted alongside John—not for the exact same reason, but for a very similar one.

Latham reached into his pack and brought out a heavy block wrapped in waxed paper. "I'm warning you." He had an easy smile—too easy to trust. His fingers were long and lithe, and they undid the paper with ease.

The first whiff of the cheese was the worst. It brought to mind old socks, or perhaps corpses rotting in airless caves. John choked.

Marcelo pinched his nose shut. "Damn, man. That is *rank.*"

John managed a second whiff, and discovered that the cheese was indeed a lie. His second sniff of the cheese was even worse than the first, and how that was possible, he didn't know.

"Isn't it terrible?" Latham grinned, and picked up a knife. "It's the most useful disgusting cheese I've encountered. Tell people you're selling cheese, produce this, and suddenly everyone's eager to have you on your way. They don't even pay attention to your questions."

"Are you a liar, then?"

Latham shrugged. "Maybe. Probably? Not so much. I suppose it depends on your particular point of view." He cut a thin sliver of cheese and held it out. "Here. Want some?"

"Tastes better than it smells, does it?"

"The man I bought it from told me it was an acquired taste," Latham said. "I've yet to acquire it. I have been trying, though." He paused. "Anyone else?"

Heads shook around the fire. John made the sign to ward off the evil eye, but Latham just chuckled and carefully wrapped the cheese back up, tucking the ends of the paper into the folds.

"Here's the question," Latham said. "When I tell myself this is the most delicious cheese in the world, that I'm going to absolutely *love* it—am I *lying*? Or am I *hoping?*"

"Fantasizing," John muttered.

Latham slid the cheese in his mouth. His nose scrunched. "Still terrible. I've not acquired the taste for it yet, I see. No worries; I've six pounds of the stuff to go."

All British were odd, John reminded himself. They might seem rational, but why else would they fight so many wars, just for the dubious pleasure of ruling the ungrateful?

John shook his head and divided the soup into bowls. The bread Latham produced was good, at least—soft on the inside with a crisp, flaky crust.

For a while, they didn't speak—*a while* being approximately ninety seconds, during which their mouths were occupied with spoons and soup.

Then Latham snapped his fingers. "Bugger it," he said. "I've spent *days* thinking of this moment, and the instant it arrives, all I can talk about is cheese, cheese, cheese. Good heavens; what is wrong with me?"

It was a very good question. John had no idea.

Latham turned to him. "You saved my life. I am in your debt. How can I ever repay you?"

John was not going to roll his eyes at this particular specimen of drama. Who *said* that sort of thing to another human?

Latham apparently thought the same thing, because he frowned, tapping one forefinger against his thin, pale lips. "You know," he mused, "in all the stories, they never mention how utterly *awkward* it is to say such a thing. It sounds terribly pretentious, actually. I assure you, I have very few pretensions. Maybe one of them. Two of them. I am a regular bundle of anti-pretension, in fact."

John raised a single eyebrow. With *that* accent? Unlikely. Pretty British officers like him undoubtedly had more than a few pretensions.

"I'm making things worse, aren't I?"

John nodded.

"Well, then. Is there anything I can do for you?"

It was, perhaps, irrational to feel angry under the circumstances. Here was this man, with his cheese and his smile, sitting before him, offering his help.

It wasn't as if John didn't *need* help; he did, in fact, a thousand times over. His last letter from his sister, Lizzie, six months past, had spoken of trouble at home. *Now that Noah's freed, people don't want us here.* Every week in which no further correspondence arrived diminished his ability to make excuses. Something was wrong, and the only reason

John wasn't in a tearing panic was that tearing panics had never accomplished a damned thing. Here he was, in Virginia, with his sister and mother five hundred miles away.

He'd fought. He'd survived. Damn it, he ought to be able to go home.

Home might no longer exist.

He needed help. He needed a goddamned legion of soldiers to put down whatever unrest his family faced. He needed constables who cared about the peace of black freedmen, and not just the whispers of their white comrades. He needed laws that would protect the ones he loved.

All he had were his own two hands, and one of them was presently in a sling.

A true offer of help would have been welcome. But this one? This offer wasn't honestly meant. Any of the things John desperately needed were off the table.

This man didn't want to help; he wanted a handshake. Even that was off the table; after they'd parted ways, John had stupidly injured his right shoulder tripping over a rock on the way up the redoubt. Latham wanted a modicum of reassurance that he was a decent fellow.

John's shoulder hurt. He was too tired to reassure anyone, let alone pretty British officers with undisclosed pretensions.

John exhaled slowly. "I know how this dance is supposed to work. I say there's nothing I can think of. You press me to think of something; I demur, because we both know you don't really mean it. We shake hands, or I try to"—he gestured with his head to the sling—"and you leave, convinced you've done everything possible."

"Is *that* how it's supposed to go?" Henry looked at him with wide eyes. "That's a good bit more fleshed out than my list."

John ignored him. "It turns out that I'm tired. Nobody ever taught me which fork to use, and I ran out of etiquette somewhere around the time I was trying not to lose my toes at Valley Forge. I *do* need something, and I don't care about pinning a polite little medal saying, 'Well, at least you tried' on your shoulder."

"You Americans *have* medals saying that?"

John stopped, shaking his head. "No. Of course we don't. It's figurative."

"Of course it is. Pardon the interruption. You were going to tell me what you needed."

"I—" Latham really *was* rather odd. John paused, regrouping. He almost felt like a bit of a heel doing this, but—

"I'm taking my leave of the army tomorrow," he said. It had taken a bit of negotiation, that, but the doctor hadn't known if he would recover the use of his arm. John had been desperate to go home, to find his family; the Continental Army was counting the cost of soldiers lying about doing nothing while the peace accords started.

"They've no need for an injured soldier, and I may never be able to use my arm." John, in fact, believed no such thing. He had exaggerated the pain with the express purpose of convincing the doctor to declare him officially an invalid. He had to get home.

"I have a long journey ahead of me. Anyone who might otherwise accompany me on the road is either white or dead. And—" No. He wasn't about to disclose his worries about his family to this man.

"Right. Is that it?"

"Is that *it*?" John echoed. "I'm going on foot. There are bandits on the road. We'll be living off the land as we move, so I hope you know how to set traps." He glanced at the man. "I hope you have a taste for squirrel meat, too. It's rather late in the year."

"Where is your home, then?"

"Rhode Island," John said pointedly.

"Ha, I guessed right!"

"It's some five hundred, maybe six hundred miles distant," John said repressively.

Latham folded his arms. Right. Here it came. The polite refusal.

"Sounds better than selling cheese," the other man said. "When do we leave?"

John blinked and looked over at the man. He was sitting contentedly in place, breaking the crust of his bread into pieces. The firelight made his hair seem even more orange than it had before. He didn't look as if he was lying.

He had to be lying. He didn't mean it.

"Tomorrow morning," John said in slow disbelief. "You understand that people like me aren't…loved in these parts? We'll move fast. We'll have no luxuries. I have no money to speak of."

A tiny frown touched Latham's face. *Finally*. It had taken long enough to put him off. But instead of protesting and suddenly discovering he had other things to do, Latham just bowed his head and considered his soup bowl.

"Well. That makes my head hurt all over again. Does that not make your head hurt?"

John looked over at Marcelo, who shook his head in equal confusion.

"You can't *say* the cheese is delicious and not eat the cheese," Latham muttered. "It's just not done."

Maybe he caught their disbelieving stares, because he smiled helplessly. "It makes sense inside my head," he said. "Or rather—it *doesn't* make sense, that's the entire point. I swear to you, I'm not as stupid as I appear."

"I see," John said, even though he didn't.

"But look at me," Henry said. "My father used to say I was empty-headed, but I assure you, it's not true—quite the opposite, in fact. There's too *much* in my head, not too little.

Pretend I never said anything. I meant to ask—what time shall I meet you, then?"

"Have you ever traveled thirty miles in a day?" John demanded. "Day after day, all in a row?"

"Of course." Latham looked almost indignant.

"On foot?"

"Ah…" A beat of hesitation. "Well… Not exactly? But I'm quite capable, really. Don't worry about me. Sunrise—will that do?"

"Sunrise is fine," John said in disbelief.

"Right. Then I shouldn't dawdle. I've a great deal to do in preparation. I'll see you then."

"Right," John echoed scornfully. He watched the other man leave with a shake of his head.

"What *was* that?" Marcelo asked.

"I don't know," John said, "but even odds, he'll not arrive in the morning. At any rate, prissy fellow like him—he'll beg off ten miles into the journey, complaining of blisters."

Marcelo nodded his head in agreement. "Lord above," he finally said. "I will never understand humanity. People are *strange*."

"Hmm." Latham's figure disappeared into the darkening night. John sighed. "Something tells me this one is particularly queer."

~

"Good day!"

John had taken his leave from camp. He'd carefully shaken the left hands of the men with whom he'd spent years cooking squirrels and stones into soup. Captain Olney had given him a nod and a final good-bye. Colonel Hamilton—with whom John had spent less than twelve hours on the battlefield—had clapped his good shoulder and made another idle promise—"If ever you're in need, let me know and I'll put my name to use to offer some assistance."

John had left the Continental Army encampment an hour after sunrise. By the time he walked out the gate, he'd managed to forget Latham—completely—again.

But here he was, standing next to the road, arms folded and smiling brightly. "It *is* a nice day, isn't it?"

John stared stupidly at him, it being too early in the morning for this level of explosive cheerfulness.

"How are you doing this fine morning, John?" He came over and clapped a hand against John's shoulder. Pain shot through him like lightning.

John didn't wince. He didn't even let himself shiver. Instead, he brought his good hand up, catching the other man's wrist, yanking it away from his shoulder.

Their eyes met.

Touching a white man like this, in reprimand... Not a good idea.

Latham didn't *look* likely to burst into violence, no matter what had been said about him on the battlefield, but then, you never could tell with some of these fancy types. Some of them could go from laughter to the most violent rage in the blink of an eye. It wouldn't matter that John had saved his life. It wouldn't matter if John had been his *brother*. John was black; Latham was white. And if Latham was one of *those*— one who would take offense at the slightest hint that he needed to treat John as human—then it was just as well John find out now.

"Not that shoulder," John said.

"Oh." Latham's eyes widened. "I am *such* an idiot. I had forgotten, and the sling is under your jacket..."

"Don't want everyone on the road thinking me an easy mark." John looked at him. "Not the other shoulder, either."

Latham frowned.

"It's not wounded," John explained. "I'm just not one for giving or receiving punches in various spots of my body to demonstrate my manhood."

"Oh. A handshake then?" Latham extended his arm.

It would be boorish to brush that off, and in all honesty, John was beginning to suspect that Latham was something of a puppy—earnest, exuberant, and utterly devoid of house-training. John sighed. Latham's shoes looked far too fashionable for a journey of five hundred miles. He'd quit in a day, two at the most.

Very well. John could handle anything for a day, even a puppy.

He held out his left hand. Gingerly, awkwardly, their hands met. Latham's gloves were some sort of soft leather against John's bare calluses.

"Well. No point dawdling."

"We're off," Latham said. "This is so exciting! I've never been on a walking trip, did you know?"

A *walking* trip, as if this were a jaunt through the woods for pleasure. He'd last three hours at best.

"Although, that's not true, come to think of it. I walked thirty-five miles to my gran's house when I was twelve and was scolded roundly. So, ha, perhaps I have a little experience. Although that took two days."

John glanced over. Latham kept going.

"*She* didn't scold me, mind—it was my father, and I suppose the dean, who seemed to think a trip to my grandmother's was superfluous when I had a Latin examination. As if avoiding the Latin examination were not the very point of the trip! Ah well. Sic transit gloria Henry."

John just shook his head at him.

"That's all the Latin I remember now, so maybe the dean had a point? But then, I've never needed to know Latin, so maybe I also had a point too. What did he suppose would happen?"

John did not hazard an answer. He wasn't sure who the *he* in that sentence was, and he didn't want to ask.

"If ruffians descend upon us and demand that I conjugate Latin verbs, I will be unable to save us by means of quick thinking," Henry said. "I apologize for my failures in advance. I also, however, will apologize to the ruffians, because I cannot imagine what sort of heartbreaking childhood would lead them to make such bizarre demands. Ah, maybe we'd have something in common! Come to think of it…"

Latham was going to give up. Any mile now, he'd beg off. And even if he didn't, if John didn't say anything, Latham would have to stop talking. *Eventually.*

He would, wouldn't he?

~

Latham did not stop talking.

Not that morning. Not that night, as he asked about John's shoulder and if cold compresses helped, and if they didn't, if hot compresses did. He talked as he prepared some kind of a…thing…of cloth and herbs and warm heat over the fire for John. He talked as they ate and offered John bread and disgusting cheese.

John took the bread.

He talked the next morning—more cheese, more bread, more stories about goats and chickens and his father, whom he did not like, and his mother, whom he did. He did not stop talking.

Not that night. Not the next morning, nor the morning after, nor even the morning after that. John had imagined that Henry Latham would complain of hunger, weariness, thirst, and general malcontent.

Had John been given more than a few minutes to think the matter over, he might have realized that a man who greeted a nighttime assailant with "nice weather for a siege?" was unlikely to be a complainer.

He was just as unlikely to be silent.

He talked.

And he talked.

And he *talked*.

After the first few days, John had resorted to the desperate measure of not responding to even direct questions—not a nod of the head, not a grunt, not so much as a commiserating glance out of the corner of his eye—in order to satisfy his own curiosity about how long it would take Latham to run out of words.

Four days since they'd started their journey, and Latham was still going.

It had become a battle of wills: Latham wanted to engage John in conversation, and John refused to give in. Latham talked through the entirety of one day. Then the next. He talked until Virginia was gone, and Maryland, with its almost bare forests and its red, crunchy leaves underfoot, stretched before them.

Latham talked and talked, and one week into their journey, John realized he had made a grave error in his calculations: Latham talked, and John didn't hate it.

CHAPTER THREE

Henry Latham was all too aware that John Hunter seemed to be engaged in a heroic battle to avoid conversation. He'd managed to set up camp for two nights running without saying a word.

He hadn't complained when Henry had brought out the cheese.

"Here," Henry said, holding a slice of death-smelling cheese out to him. "Have some!"

A shift of Hunter's eyes out to the horizon was his only response.

"Day nine," Henry said. "I am eating the cheese. The cheese *will* be delicious. It will be amazingly delicious. It will positively melt in my mouth."

He put the slice on his tongue. It tasted like feet and frog shit. Henry choked, coughing, and reached for his tin flask of water.

Across from him, John tried very hard not to smile.

"Alas. The cheese prevails once again," Henry said. "The taste is not yet acquired. Ah, well. Tomorrow is a new day."

John just looked at him.

"You really should try the cheese," Henry said. "You seem like the sort of open-minded fellow who would find…something to love in this cheese."

John's mouth opened, then clapped shut. *Such* a valiant effort.

Futile, but valiant. From long experience, Henry knew that he was highly unlikely to shut up, not for any reason. He wasn't made for silence.

Nobody was, really. Henry had once been told—perhaps by one of the tutors whom his father had hired to try to make him a sober, learned fellow and who instead had been inexorably pulled into a lengthy discussion of some arcane, unimportant point of history—that resisting him was like trying to hold the ocean in place with one's fingers. It wouldn't work, and the ocean (if it felt anything about the matter, which it might, because who knew what oceans thought about? Not Henry, although he could speculate) regarded the effort with nothing so much as amusement.

They were three miles out of Philadelphia, one early morning, when Mr. Hunter finally gave in.

He stopped dead in his tracks.

He turned to Henry. He rubbed his head with his free hand. His hair was growing from short, tight curls into medium tight curls, not yet so long that they could be put into disarray. He glanced at Henry and finally spoke.

"Do you ever get tired of talking?" he demanded.

Henry gave him a delightful smile. "You lasted so long! Twelve entire days—really, I'm so impressed! That was excellent. Utterly excellent!"

Hunter narrowed his eyes at him. "What do you mean?"

"I wish we had those little medals you were talking about earlier," Henry said appreciatively.

"What? What medals?"

"The tin ones. The ones that said 'Well, at least you tried.'

I would award you one right now. You definitely deserve it, don't you think?"

Hunter gave him an unblinking stare. For a moment, he tilted his head, as if trying to make sense of what Henry was saying. Henry could have told him there was no point in that either.

"You didn't answer my question," Hunter said. "Do you ever get *tired* of talking?"

Right. Henry had been so delighted at the fact of a question that he'd forgotten to answer.

"What an excellent question." He considered it now. "Tired of talking? What an odd idea. Let me check." The possibility had honestly never occurred to Henry. The back of his throat tickled—just a hint of incipient soreness, not enough to bother him—and if they hadn't passed a creek a mile or so back, his mouth would be dry. He tentatively tested his tongue, moving it in his mouth from side to side. His feet were a little sore. His tongue? No signs of fatigue at all.

"No." He cast a bright smile at his walking companion. "I don't believe I do. Is there a reason you ask?"

Mr. Hunter had been—over the past week or so—slowly losing his touch. The repressive look he gave Henry was scarcely forbidding. He looked as if he was on the verge of smiling.

Oh, he tried not to react to a thing Henry said. But he had failed. Henry had been counting Hunter's smiles. He was at four thus far this morning.

"Simple curiosity," Mr. Hunter said. He shook his head and started walking once more. "Thus far this morning, you've covered the finer points of piquet strategy, the musical oeuvre of Handel, and the various gaits of horses along with their utility in exacerbating lower back pain. It's not even midday. Aren't you afraid you'll run out of words?

Or ideas?"

"Not in the least." Henry glanced over at Mr. Hunter. "I should warn you, I'm a talkative sort."

"I had surmised that to be the case sometime over the last hour or hundred."

"If it bothers you, I can keep quiet."

"Really? In that case..." The man seemed to be considering that as if it were a real possibility.

"I only meant for a minute, maybe two. I always forget that I'm supposed to be doing it," Henry added.

Hunter's lip twitched. "I knew the offer was too good to be true."

"Personally, I find that conversation works much better when two are involved. Haven't you anything to say?"

Hunter's eyebrows went down in contemplation, as if perhaps, he *did* have something—*one* thing—to say.

"Here," Henry said. "I'll give you some space to think."

"You will?"

"Of course!" Henry did his best to do something entirely unfamiliar: He tried to shut up.

Their strides lifted dust along the road, little plumes of light brown. Light brown. Now *that* was a nice color. Months ago, he'd marched through something red and claylike. It had caked his boots and stained his trousers—permanently, it turned out—thus ruining all hope he had of keeping his sharp appearance in the field. He wondered if that clay would make a good dye. Possibly. Probably. Definitely, if one could apply the stain evenly. He'd heard about dyes once. In fact—

"Did you know that beetroot—"

"That wasn't even a minute!" Hunter was laughing.

"Oh damn. I forgot! I was waiting for you to respond. You were going to do it this time, too!"

"What could I have said to any of your conversation

earlier? I don't know much about piquet," Hunter finally said. "I've not had so many opportunities to play cards for money."

"In the infantry, you haven't? Well, good heavens. No wonder Britain was defeated. The Continental Army possesses far more discipline than I thought possible."

"I'm not precisely representative of the entire army." Hunter rolled his eyes. "As a personal matter, I choose not to risk what I have."

"Look at you, all reasonable and conservative with your funds." Henry drew back to punch the other man in the shoulder.

Hunter looked back at him repressively.

"Ah, right. You don't like that. I'd forgotten." He let his hand drop. "I'll try to remember. Definitely. If I can."

"Mmm. At least try to make it believable when you say it?"

Henry shrugged and made a mental note to definitely try to remember. "Ah. Well. So let's not talk of piquet. What topic of conversation would you introduce?"

Mr. Hunter frowned.

"You can answer 'no conversation,' but then I shall just choose whatever flits into my head, and I have to tell you, that's a dreadfully mixed bag."

"I can't make you out," Hunter finally said. "When we first…ah…met…?"

"You mean when you tried to kill me?"

Hunter grimaced.

"Was it impolite to bring that up?" Henry tilted his head. "Oh dear. We can't let that come between us. You were doing your patriotic duty, and—as an observer who had more than a little reason to care about the outcome—I must say that up until the final moments, you did a commendable job of doing me in. Very good. You were very good at killing me."

"Not good enough. Are you capable of having a straightforward conversation? One that starts at the beginning and continues on in a straight line to the conclusion?"

Henry considered that. "Yes," he finally said, "but it has to be a very short line." He held up two fingers a raisin's width apart to demonstrate the precise duration of his focus. "I do tend to go off a bit. My father always used to shake me by the collar when I was young. 'Focus!' he'd shout in my ear. Then I'd forget everything altogether. But what were we talking about? Killing. Patriotism. Oh—right—you started by saying that you couldn't make me out. Good heavens. I was an utter cad in response. You introduced a perfectly acceptable topic of conversation, one about which I have particular knowledge, and I just went straight off onto some other ridiculous thing, as if I were a horse spooked by a spider."

"*Are* horses spooked by—no, never mind."

"Yes," Henry said consolingly. "You're getting the picture. It's best not to ask questions around me if you don't actually want them answered, I'm afraid."

"I have always been accounted a fast learner."

"So let us return to your original question. You wanted to ask about me. This is an excellent conversational theme. I know almost nothing about arachnids, not that I would ever let that stop me from expounding on them, but I know a great deal about me."

"I thought you were…" Hunter bit his lip, searching for a word. "That night, I thought you were despairing, perhaps. And yet here you are. I would almost call you…an idealist, maybe. You hardly seem the sort to *want* to die. Why didn't you want to go back to England?"

A cold shadow touched Henry's heart. He smiled brightly through that shadow and reached for the first semiplausible explanation that came to mind.

"You can't be that fast a learner," he scoffed instead. "I

would have thought my reason to be obvious. That would be the treason."

"The what?"

"The treason," Henry repeated. "You know. Treachery? Aiding the enemy? The complete opposite, on my part, of the patriotic duty that you seem to have in such abundance? The treason is why I do not want to go back to England."

Hunter was staring at him. "I don't understand."

Henry didn't have the words to explain everything in his heart, and so he reached for easier words, ones he could utilize.

"It's not that difficult a concept. Think the consequences through for a moment. The treason would be such a bloody mess. Trials, beheadings. Blood everywhere. My mother would weep, my family would be launched into scandal, my sister's husband would become even more of a bore—which I would not have thought possible, but every time I think he's reached the utter zenith of monotony, he exceeds the physical limits of tedium once again. You know. Treason is just damned hard on everyone all around."

"I understand that," Hunter said. "But...treason?"

"What do you think I was doing at the redoubt? Following orders?"

"Well..."

"No. I thought to myself that it was an *excellent* night for a siege. Then Fusiliers Redoubt went up, and I thought it was an excellent night for a feint, too. I was afraid I was going to blurt it out in front of everyone, so I went to hide."

John looked at him. "Why?"

"You are not seriously asking *why* I thought I might say anything flitting through my head after this many days in my company, are you?"

"No—why didn't you *say* anything?"

"Oh, that. After I read the circular, I had to do *something,* even if the something I did was nothing. Up until that point, I'd managed to hide my treason in incompetence. 'Oh, you meant *that* left' works once, and 'didn't you say advance at *three* drum strokes?' I ran the most inept company in the entire British army, and my men loved me. We so rarely saw battle."

"You…didn't want to fight?"

"I told you it was treason."

"Well, but…"

"Technically, I'm not sure it *was* actually treason—possibly, my behavior at the moment was just a cause for court-martial—but purposefully evading orders and absconding from my position still brings us back around to willful disobedience and desertion. Which means weeping, scandal, boorish husbands, et cetera and so forth." Henry swept his arms wide. "I use the word 'treason' as a sort of shorthand for all of that. I prefer to live, all things considered, but if death is inevitable, I'd rather my family think me bravely, stupidly heroic."

If anything, Hunter looked more confused. His eyebrows drew together in a dark line. His mouth squished up.

"You are an incredibly odd individual."

"I know," Henry said. "It's my saving grace. People tell me all the time I'm a queer fellow, but if I'm going to talk as much as I do, I might as well give them something interesting to listen to, don't you think?"

"Mmm."

"My father hated it. He always wished I would keep my mouth shut. Stand in one place. Stop chattering about everything, or he'd knock me—" Henry stopped talking. Pasted a smile on his face. "Good thing I was a second son and he didn't have to actually succeed in reforming me! They tried me on all the second son things—law, church, you name it—and finally gave up and tossed me into the army. He'll be glad

I'm dead." He considered this. "Honestly, I'm glad to be dead, too. The best solution to an awful mess; I had thought so for months, but hadn't quite figured out how to die without actually *dying,* a disfavored outcome, until you came along."

"That—it seems—perhaps excessive?"

"Ah, you'd agree if you knew him. He's a terrible father. The absolute *worst.* You couldn't imagine."

Hunter looked at him. "The man who fathered me owned me and my mother. He never beat me, but he did sell my mother when he gambled himself into a hard spot."

Henry felt his mouth go dry. He thought of his father yelling at him. Telling him to focus. Telling him to make something of himself, goddamn it, and…

"You win," he said. "You win. That is definitely worse."

"I had not realized we were playing a game. Do I get a medal saying 'You *didn't* try' now? Had I any choice in the matter, I assure you this is not a game I would strive to succeed at."

"Had you any choice in the matter, what would you have done, if not soldiering? If you were allowed to choose? Would you have gone to university?"

Hunter stared at him. "Are you completely ignorant of the world?" he finally asked. "I mean this honestly. Is something wrong with you? Did your father hit you too many times? University? In what world could I *choose* to go to university?"

Henry wasn't going to flush. He wasn't going to feel stupid—even though, apparently, he was an idiot of the most gargantuan proportions. "Ah. Um. This…hypothetical one, now? Where you could choose anything you wanted? Anything at all?"

Hunter rolled his eyes. "Good. Then I choose to be independently wealthy."

"An excellent choice, if I do say so myself."

"Nobody would sell my family." That was said on a growl.

"I wouldn't ever have to worry about where they were, what they were doing, if they were alive."

"That seems like a...very good start. What would you do with all your wealth, though?"

Hunter looked at him.

"It's just a question! You could, I suppose, allow it to lie in a bank and make interest of some kind, or you could use it for...oh, I don't know, saving starving dogs? Educating orphans?"

"Is that what fancy British officers do with their wealth?" Hunter asked.

Latham felt himself flush. "I wouldn't know," he lied. "My father was...a...tailor."

Hunter raised one eyebrow at that rather obvious lie, and just shook his head. "Well." There was a pointedness to his words as he spoke. "If I were born a second son—and I suppose, in a sense, I was, although my father's first son would never have acknowledged such a thing—with all the attendant wealth that came with that, I would have gone into trade."

"Into trade." Henry felt dazed. "You'd have gone into trade."

"Of course." Hunter gave him a nod. "I grew up in a ship-yard in South Carolina, you know. I used to listen to the traders talk in the shipyard—they never did notice me, even when I was right there—talking about their money and where it came from and where they'd get more of it. They'd find people in Africa, bring them to the Caribbean or the South, where they'd trade them for rum or sugar or cotton. Back to England, where they'd sell that for manufactured goods... It always made me think."

"You wanted to trade people?"

"No. They all seemed to have a want of imagination—trading the same things as everyone else. I wanted to show you didn't have to trade in human flesh, or the products of human flesh. I used to lie in bed at night and imagine a world where I stole one of the ships and made more money than the rest of them doing the things they'd failed to imagine."

"That sounds like a noble aim," Henry managed to say. Nobler than anything he'd ever thought of.

"Noble, ha." Hunter pressed the fingers of his left hand to his forehead, shutting his eyes momentarily. "I've learned long since to hope for smaller things, attainable things. I want my sister to be well. I want her husband not to be enslaved. I want to live with my family and not be separated from them except by my own choices."

The light in his eyes dimmed somewhat, but the fervor in his voice deepened. "I ask for what I can get. There's no room for childish dreams in my life."

"But those aren't childish dreams. I rather liked them."

Hunter wrinkled his nose as if annoyed that he'd spoken. "They're childish. Do you think that anyone would do business with someone who aimed to rewrite the way trading was done in its entirety?"

"Maybe," Henry said earnestly, "if you picked the right name. You could fool everyone. Pick something grandiose sounding, and they might not notice. Something like…"

"'Just the Usual Sort of Traders, Don't Mind Us' lacks a certain ring."

"No, something simple and ridiculous-sounding, like 'Lord Traders.' Who would think that *they* would be up to anything sneaky?"

Hunter sighed. "Forget I said anything."

For a moment, Henry tried. He looked over at Hunter, walking along at a regular clip. His injured arm was still bound to his chest in a sling; they'd checked it every night, and every night, Hunter hissed in pain when he attempted motion. Maybe his dreams were childish. Maybe they should be set aside. Still, it had sounded better than any idea that Henry had ever had thus far, and Henry had a great many ideas.

"Sorry. I can't. You see, we are...very, very different, of course. But I think we are of a similar bent."

"Oh?" Hunter was better at looking dubious than any man Henry had ever met. He could communicate disbelief in one syllable, with just a tiny hint of emphasis.

Henry was even better at ignoring those signs. "You ought to have asked me *why* I was committing treason. It wasn't on a whim. I *speak* on a whim; I commit treason with deadly seriousness."

Hunter just raised an eyebrow, and that absence of suspicion was more than enough invitation to expound.

"You see, around one year ago, I found this paper. It was trash. Some revolutionary rubbish that someone had nailed to the walls of a barn to annoy us. I made the mistake of reading it."

"I can imagine what it was like. Bombastic. Full of derision for your sort."

"No, no. It wasn't, that's the thing. It's still in my pocket," Henry said softly. "I memorized the parts that mattered to me. *We hold these truths to be self-evident. That all men are created equal.*" Those words had shattered him. He'd read them over and over, again and again, shaking them up and down inside his head. They had *hurt*, making his head ache as he tried to put them in their place. He'd tried to drown them out with chatter. With other ideas.

But that was the thing about Henry's mind. It never settled on any one idea for any length of time, but it always came swirling back to the thoughts that could seduce him day after day. Night after night.

All men are created equal, they'd whispered. *All men are created equal. Even you.*

Hunter flicked a look at him. "That sounds like the Declaration of Independence. It meant something to you? It shouldn't have. It's just a string of pretty words."

"It's *not*," Henry said hotly. "Those are *ideals*."

A dismissive wave of the other man's hand. "Thomas Jefferson owns people. He no more thinks that *all* men are equal than the King of England does. It's all just words. That Declaration is nothing but ink on parchment, put there to make poorer men risk their lives so that Jefferson can pay less than his damned share of taxes."

"Well, they may be words, but they worked." Henry folded his arms. "An ideal set in motion is a dangerous thing. You can't control who believes it, or whether they take it to heart. 'All men are created equal.' Think of the power of that phrase."

"I have," Hunter said curtly. "'All men.' Ha. Tell me, when you were mulling over the equality of men up in your redoubt, did you ever imagine a man like me?"

Henry raised his head. He looked into Hunter's eyes—dark, in the warmer brown of his face. Fierce. Unrelenting.

He swallowed. He wanted to lie. To say that of course he had thought of *all* men. But... He was many, many things. Including a liar. He was definitely a liar. But lying now wouldn't just be pointless babble. It would be *wrong*.

He shut his eyes. "No. I didn't."

Hunter just shrugged. "Of course not." He said it quietly, with no bitterness.

He *should* have been bitter. He should have been angry. When people talked about all men, they should think about him.

And that made Henry think. And think. And think. And think some more.

43

CHAPTER FOUR

T he impossible had happened: Henry Latham had shut up.

John hadn't thought such a thing would ever happen, but there he was—quiet for hours. He didn't speak when they stopped at a stream, dipping tin cups into cold water that tasted like stone and moss. He didn't speak throughout their late afternoon snack of dry bread and hard jerky.

Instead, he fiddled with an iron ring that he'd pulled from his pack, turning it around in his hands over and over.

Consider the equality of the black man, apparently, was a mental exercise that had left even Latham tongue-tied. No surprise; most people were easily befuddled when their cheerful principles overran their prejudice.

He didn't speak again until they came up on an inn just before twilight. Then, as John didn't spare a glance to the stone chimneys whose wisps of smoke promised heat, he stopped in the road.

"It's been a while," he said. "We've been sleeping on the

ground for almost two weeks. Have you ever thought about halting somewhere for a night?"

Oh, Latham was so naïve. He was pretty, in the way of pretty men who knew they were pretty: high cheekbones, flushed from the day's exertion; smooth, bright hair pulled back in a fashionable club. His eyelashes flashed at John—not in so much as a bat but in the desperate entreaty of a tired man.

They'd made twenty-seven miles today, and he was no doubt tired.

"At an inn?" John made a face. "Hardly worth the coin."

"Uh. Coin isn't..." Latham flushed even brighter. "I have a bit on me, as it happens. I should think that a room at an inn..."

"Two rooms," John said. "That's what they'll be willing to give us. More like one room and a berth in the stables, if I'm lucky."

Latham understood his point immediately.

"Nonsense. You're sharing your journey; I'm sharing what I have. Any particularity on my part was lost during the last years at war."

John felt his nose wrinkle. "Who was your father again?"

"Um." Latham's eyes screwed shut. "A...man? A potter. Right. He made pots."

He'd been a tailor before. The truth was more like neither. With that talk of university? With the officer's braid John had seen on his shoulder that night? Unlikely. Even more unlikely with his mention of being a second son with the *usual* choice of law, church, or army.

Potter's son, John's good backside. What kind of potter's son developed any sort of particularity about sharing his room in the first place? Didn't matter, though. John had known the man was a liar from the first evening.

Instead, he jerked a thumb at the inn. "They will care in

there. They'll let me stay in your room, but only if you pretend I'm your servant. And I'm not."

Latham's mouth scrunched together. He stared at the stone building, as if imagining the warm rooms inside. A cold breeze brought with it the scent of something savory—stew, perhaps, and John heard the other man's stomach gurgle. "We'll see about that." So saying, he marched in the direction of the inn.

He was going to get both their heads bashed in. John sighed, then followed.

Latham marched into the inn with the air of a man who owned the place.

The man who *actually* owned the place, a balding man wearing a stained apron, brightened when he caught sight of him.

"Sir," he said, completely ignoring John, "a thousand welcomes to you. You have the look of one who has been involved in the war. Officer?"

"Indeed," Latham said jovially. It was, John supposed, not entirely a lie. He *had* been in the war. He *had* been an officer. He just didn't mention that he'd fought for the other side.

The innkeeper bowed distinctly. "Thank you for your service, sir. How can I help you?"

"My good man. A room, if you please." Latham's manners had changed. They were like glistening icicles hanging from the eaves—cold and perfectly formed. Glancing at the tables nearby, he added, "Dinner as well. Your goodwife appears to set an excellent table."

The innkeeper nodded. "Of course, of course, sir. If you could come over here?" He gestured to John. "Your master's luggage—"

Latham tilted his head. "My pardon! I thought that was clear when we entered. Corporal Hunter here is no servant. We were comrades-in-arms."

"Former corporal," John muttered. "Now no longer in the infantry."

The innkeeper paused. He frowned at Latham. He glanced at his dining area.

"I've just a pack," Latham continued. "I'll take it up myself. But I'd like to wash and have dinner. If you could direct us—"

"I'll hold a table for you, sir, but your, ah…"

"Hunter is his name. And he is my traveling companion." John winced.

"Your companion may eat with the servants, if you please. And we have a place in the stables for him."

"It doesn't please. It doesn't please at all."

"It's not negotiable. I must think of the comfort of my other guests."

Latham frowned.

It wouldn't take him long to give up his principles. It never did. Rationality said that Latham could get his warm room and dinner, and if John couldn't… Well, it wasn't *Latham's* fault, was it? There was no principle so fine that it could stand up to a dish of warm stew at a comfortable table after a twenty-seven-mile walk.

Latham shook his head, let out a gusty sigh, and turned to John. "Well, Hunter." Their eyes met, and John did not look away. If Latham was going to abandon him for a warm bed, he'd not give the man the satisfaction of backing down. "You win."

"This game." John shook his head. "I really hate winning this game, and yet I find myself continually dragooned into playing."

Latham sighed. "Do we eat with the servants and bunk in the stables, or continue on?"

"We?"

Latham gave him a quirk of a smile. "I'm too overcome with exhaustion to make a decision. It's in your hands."

John met his eyes. Latham was a liar, and—by his own admission—a traitor. But he'd asked for his opinion.

And so instead, John shrugged. "I suppose tonight we can bunk in the stables. You'll toughen eventually, but for now, we'll compromise in deference to your softness."

"Excellent."

Latham turned to the innkeeper. "Dinner for two, then. With the servants."

~

Latham got them a private corner to wash, and, after the innkeeper grimaced at the thought of an officer —a *white* officer—eating with the servants, a table in the back of the kitchen with stew for them both.

The innkeeper was even—almost—apologetic to Latham when he conducted them out to the stable. "Should be warm enough in the hayloft," he said, as they climbed the rickety ladder. "We've a full complement of horses tonight."

It was warm. The hay poked through the blankets they unrolled but it was—in a relative sense—the most comfortable that John had been on this journey.

Their bedrolls were inches apart, meaning that in the gloom, when John turned over, he saw Latham looking back at him.

Those damned eyelashes. Pretty was pretty. It didn't mean a damned thing at all, except that the random conformation of features that nature had endowed Latham with were, on balance, pleasing to the eye.

"How's your shoulder?"

John shrugged and unwound his sling. The doctor had said that he might recover full use of his arm, or that he might never have it. Slowly, he stretched his hand out to full extension, flaring his fingers. He could feel the answering pain in the ball of his shoulder, but it was dimming every day.

"I think," he said, "the doctor had no idea what he was talking about. It will be fine."

"Good." Henry's smile lit his face.

He was so damned pretty.

It had never bothered John that he liked looking at pretty men, no matter what churchgoers said. If he'd let the world around him decide what he ought to think of himself, he'd still be enslaved in South Carolina. Lizzie, the sister he'd raised, would be twenty-three and beautiful alongside him in slavery—if he were lucky—and sold somewhere else if he were not. If he'd listened to everyone else, there would be nothing he could do to protect her.

Instead... He thought of her last letter, of the months and months since she'd sent it, the panic that he refused to indulge lurking at the back of his mind. *I'm coming, Lizzie. I'm coming. Just be there when I arrive.*

In truth, John had found his natural inclinations to be incredibly convenient. When he'd been just out of childhood, he'd had no desire to start a family, even though his master had suggested he do so. Loving a woman, having a child— that would have made enslavement his home. It would have been the worst thing he could have done. They'd have tied him to his master even more than his sister had, and leaving her the first time had almost broken his heart. Lucky that he had never wanted women in that way.

It was luck that he liked looking at pretty men instead. Luck that his eyes traced Henry's forehead, and he wondered what he looked like underneath that shirt.

A prickle of awareness seemed to catch deep in his throat. It had always come naturally to him, with men. Looking at them and remembering to look away. Wondering *what if...*

He couldn't help but look at Latham and wonder *what if.*

It was only natural. Latham was exceptionally beautiful, and unless the British signaled these things very differently than Americans, his inclinations ran parallel to John's. There were enough men like them; during the war, there had been times John had reached out and blindly sought comfort from a fellow soldier.

Latham, he suspected, had likely done the same.

There would be no seeking comfort between them, though, not unless he wanted things to change too much. John had a family, and who knew what trouble they were in? Every moment's delay meant precious hours when he could be with them instead. He had to make good time; he couldn't let himself become beguiled into lengthening this journey.

He felt it as instinctively as if he were still in battle, as if they were still locked in combat. It was Latham or John, Latham or John, and the stakes might no longer have been his life, but he'd promised Lizzie he would see her again, and if what he feared…

No, he couldn't think about his fears, not here, not in the darkness, not hundreds of miles away where he could do nothing about them.

"You were entirely right," Latham said softly in the dark. "I'm an inherently frivolous man, I'm afraid."

"You don't even shut up at night," John said unfairly. He *had* shut up that afternoon. Shockingly.

"I hadn't thought my principles through. If all men are created equal, it stands to reason that it includes all races. I hadn't thought about it at all until today, and I should have. You have every right to be annoyed. I had to go over the matter. It took me a bit."

"Well, then. It's good you set your mind at rest." There was a bit of a sarcastic edge to John's voice. He didn't even mean it that way; anything that distracted him from the things he'd heard about, of black families driven out in winter, no food, nowhere to go... Worrying wouldn't make it better. It just made his stomach clench. He sighed in the darkness. "I hope you sleep well."

"No, wait. I wanted to—that is, I needed to—" Latham reached out and set a hand on John's good shoulder.

John was too shocked to flinch away. Even through his undershirt, he felt that touch. A spot of warmth, a hint of nerves, sparked where the man's fingers lay.

Don't be an idiot, John.

"It's this," Latham said earnestly. "I hold these truths to be self-evident. That you were created equal. And that everyone who treated you as less debased themselves. I believe that you were endowed with unalienable rights: Life. Liberty. The pursuit of happiness. I believe that when you withdraw your consent to be governed, all men of conscience should stand by your side."

That spot blossomed into heat. They were face-to-face, inches apart, close enough that John could have leaned forward and touched Latham's lips with his own. And oh, for a moment, he wanted to do it. He wanted to forget his worries. He wanted to take everything this man offered—his principles, his person.

Ah, he thought at that unfurling emotion. *This. This. This is why I need to keep him at bay.*

He wasn't going to let go of his defenses for so small a gift as ordinary human kindness.

Life. Liberty. The pursuit of happiness. God, what he would have given for his family to have been born with the recognized right to just one of those. It hurt, having this pretty man—this treacherous liar—mouth sentiments that he'd yearned for before in the darkness of night. He wanted to reach out and lay hold of the man, to claim those lies for the truth he yearned for.

Instead, he made himself lie still. Told his overactive

nerves to quiet down. He looked in the other man's eyes, made himself concentrate on the hay poking his side until the discomfort took over his desire.

"According to you," John said, "I was born with those rights. They're not yours to give. I won't thank you for them."

"It's just…" Latham sighed. "Never mind."

"Are you done?"

"Yes," Latham said. "I…think so."

"Good." John turned around, offering the man his shoulder. "Go to sleep. We've a long ways to go."

CHAPTER FIVE

J ohn could feel sleep tugging his eyes shut, fogging his brain. The hayloft was warm; the straw was comfortable. Beside him, Latham drifted off in no time at all, a solid presence that he could sense even in the darkness. It would be all too easy to fall into a deep sleep.

But even slumber seemed a lie. To sleep with his back to another man was to take that man for his comrade. It required a certain degree of trust, and to give it unearned seemed anathema. Comfort was a freedom-stealing lie.

Life. Liberty. The pursuit of happiness. Stretching for ideals like those, well… They just made him forget that at the end of the day, he didn't know where his sister was. If she was well. If she was *alive.* There was no room for ideals in his life. There was no room for anything except fighting. Surviving.

After Latham's breaths evened out, John slipped out of the blankets, made his way down the rickety ladder by feel, found his coat, and slipped out the barn door.

It was frigid outside the barn. The stables and the two wings of the inn made a little open-sided courtyard. The moon was a slim, silver crescent overhead, providing just enough light for him to make out a stone well in the center of that space.

There were stars overhead, twinkling with a faint, mocking light.

He should just leave. The open road called to him in the gloom, beckoning him on. Latham was too soft. Yes, he'd kept up thus far, but only because John's arm had restricted his movement. He was getting better—he stretched his arm out, feeling a twinge, but it was a good twinge. He could go faster, farther, longer.

He would do anything for his mother. For Lizzie. He would do anything in his power. He just didn't know what he needed to do, and the unknown ate away at him.

He should leave. John was doing his best to avoid despair; Henry preferred to stay in inns and eat freshly baked bread by the fire.

John's master had told him once that while he didn't hold with beating his slaves, others did—and that it wasn't cruelty because black men didn't feel pain the way white men did. That, he had said, was why he always had his slaves on the most dangerous jobs in his shipyard. If they fell from the heights, or if a beam pinched their shoulder... Well, it wouldn't hurt them as much, would it? It was simple human-itarianism, his master had said.

That sentiment was bullshit of the highest order.

John felt pain. The cold of the night made his skin into miniature cobblestones. It bit into his toes. John ought to have put his shoes on before leaving the stables. The cold did nothing to alleviate the ache in the pads of his feet, that persistent throb of flesh abused by the day's journey.

He sat on the edge of the well and felt his thighs protest.

He wasn't magic; he felt pain.

Lizzie, Lizzie. I'm coming.

He felt hope, too, no matter how much life had tried to rob him of that. He'd felt it in the afternoon. He'd felt it that night, looking into Latham's eyes. He felt it now, thinking of Lizzie's last letter. Life could not be so cruel as to take his loved ones away now, not when he'd survived an entire war to come...home.

Home, such as it was. Home was Newport, a city where his family was being threatened simply because they were free and black. Some home.

Life could be so cruel.

Latham was nothing but trouble, and really, John ought to leave.

That he didn't, that he sat out here in the cold looking at the stars, letting numbness seep into his fingers... That was idiotic.

The barn door creaked. He turned.

Latham didn't say anything as he crept out. He'd brought half the blankets with him, and he wore them draped over his shoulders like a multipointed cape.

"Couldn't sleep?" he asked once he stood close by.

John nodded.

"Looking at the stars?"

John nodded again. "My mother told me that the stars were different in Africa. When she first got off the ship in Charleston, it was night, and she thought she'd been taken to hell."

Latham didn't answer.

"I recognize," John said dryly, "that the earth is round and that the stars are fixed at a great distance. I labored for a shipwright. I'm no fool."

"I had not said otherwise."

Somehow that just made John angrier. "It's really about your own feelings, you know."

"Your pardon?"

"All your talk of people being equal. It's not about me. It's about you. You want to believe all people are equal because it excuses your transgressions. You say 'all men are created equal' because back in Britain, you never questioned your tea or your sugar or your rum. You didn't ask who grew the cotton you wore. You never needed to. Your talk of equality is a sword, not an olive branch. If you say we are equals, you think I'll forget that you are complicit in the misery your kind inflicts on mine."

Latham still did not answer.

It was easier to talk this way than to think how helpless he was, how many miles still separated him from his desperation.

"All you idealists have a bit of Thomas Jefferson in you," John continued. "You fall short of your professed ideals and seek to make up the difference by condescending to those you see as beneath you. But your condescension does not make me feel equal."

Latham sat on the well next to John. He wrapped the blankets about himself, then set one elbow on his knee and his chin on his hand. Swathed in blankets as he was, it made him look like some sort of gnome.

"It's a fair criticism," he said quietly. "Very fair. In my defense, it's a new ideal for me. I'm still trying to make everything fit."

"That's a terrible defense," John replied. "Am I supposed to excuse you because it has only *recently* occurred to you that I could be on your level?"

"Also…a fair criticism." Latham frowned. "I've got these horribly awkward bits of elitist thought poking out everywhere, and I'm doing my damnedest to uncover them. It hurts my head, but clearly the situation has been, um, rather more personal to you than a little intellectual discomfort."

"Ha."

"You've been incredibly patient with me," Latham said. "I'm a horrible fumbler."

"Is that why you've agreed to accompany me? I'm nothing but a lesson to you. I suppose I'd be a valuable one at that. I'm black. I'm a former slave. If you wanted an object on whom to practice your equality, you could hardly do better."

Latham turned his head. "John."

The single syllable of his name echoed in the courtyard.

"I prefer to be addressed as Hunter."

Latham shifted toward him on the bench. "I am with you because you looked into my eyes on the battlefield and saw not an enemy but a man. You gave me your coat. I wasn't the only one who committed something like treason that night. You trusted me with your life when you could easily have taken mine."

"Idiocy," John muttered. "Utter idiocy."

"Empathy," Latham said. "I hold these truths to be self-evident, John. That all men are created equal. And yes, you're right. It *is* about my feelings. I desperately want to believe that I have the capacity, the right, to have everything that I've never dreamed possible. That even I—strange, odd, treasonous me, the Henry who can never focus on one thought long enough to finish a conversation—deserve happiness."

John didn't answer.

"Maybe that is selfishness," Latham said. "But then, maybe an ideal is nothing more than selfishness writ large. Caring for someone else with the hope that if you do, someone will in turn care for you. Maybe my ideals only feel so intense because my hope is so desperate."

"Ha," John said. "What do you know of desperation?"

"I don't. I don't know. But right now, I have blankets and you are freezing. If you are going to sit outside fretting, I can do something about that. Come here."

John looked over at the other man.

"I have no nicety of principle," Latham said. "I was in the infantry for years. I don't mind sharing body heat." His voice dropped. "In point of fact… I rather like it."

Strange. Odd. Treasonous. They were confusing words to come from a man who exhibited all the trappings of wealth. Not so confusing, perhaps, if that man had listened to churchgoers talk about men who liked men, the way John had not.

"Come here." Latham gestured. "Stop freezing."

John let out a breath. So. Latham had wondered *what if*, too.

It didn't change anything. John refused to think of the other man that way. He wasn't going to let the contact, thigh on thigh, mean anything when Latham shifted six inches over. He was going to ignore everything when Henry —*Latham*, he meant—put his arm around him, arranging the blankets over the two of them like a little tent.

"Your fingers are ice." It sounded like Latham was scolding.

"Sorry, I'll keep them to myself."

"Nonsense." Latham's hands pressed around his, swallowing him in warmth. "What would be the point of that when I've warmth enough for two? You have to take care of yourself." The man *was* scolding. "You've several hundred some odd miles to travel still, and here you are, freezing yourself in the middle of the night and not sleeping. Sleep is necessary to recover from injury. How are you supposed to manage your distance tomorrow, and the day after, if you keep on like this?"

John didn't answer. Latham shifted again, pressing their thighs more firmly together.

What if John were to kiss him?

Latham, he was sure, would manage to talk through it, somehow.

His lips would be warm and his skin would be rough, but *God*, he'd know how to use his tongue.

Good thing there was never going to be a what-if between them.

"If you're going to fret," Latham said, "for God's sake, man, do it in a way that doesn't hurt yourself."

Latham's arm crept around his waist, a warm bar.

"You're a regular furnace," John heard himself say.

"Nonsense. We burn at the same temperature, didn't you know? I learned that from the camp doctor. It's not so surprising, after all. We have the same flesh, with the same ability to conduct heat and cold. I'm not naturally warm. I just wasn't outside as long as you, that's all."

"Mmm." It was hard to hate a man who shared his blankets. Harder still when his hand on John's waist—steady, not importuning at all—gave John ideas that he really ought not have, not about a man he was apparently going to be traveling with for quite a while.

Equality was well and good, but...

Strange, odd, treasonous me.

But the miles went by more pleasantly when Latham was around. His chatter was amusing, John had to admit. God knew John needed to be distracted from his thoughts of the future. He served a purpose.

And for all his chatter, Latham *listened* when John spoke. He never puffed up and demanded to know why John was questioning his character. He listened to John.

What if...

Slowly, John turned his head. Leaned in, so that his nose brushed the other man's shoulder. Deliberately, he set his hand—still cold, if not as frozen as it had been—against the other man's thigh. Even through the fabric of Latham's trousers, he felt his muscles tense.

He could feel the warm exhalation of Latham's breath against his cheek, a shuddering waft of air.

Yes, he thought. *I'm here. I'm like you.*

Latham did not move. Not for moments. Not until his free hand came up and gently—ever so gently—rested on top of John's hand on his thigh. He didn't move John's hand away. Instead, he acknowledged its presence. The inappropriateness of it. The implications—what it meant for both of them—and what his acceptance meant.

They sat in silence, on the well.

Just this much, John told himself. Just this much held no meaning. It was nothing more than an acknowledgement of something they both knew. John's own inclinations had to have been obvious as well, if Latham had come out here, sat like this with him.

It meant absolutely nothing.

"You're the one who needs sleep," John finally said. "We'd best go back to…" He paused. Not *bed;* that had its hidden implications, ones he didn't want to think through at the moment. "We'd best go back to the barn, Latham."

"It's Henry. I prefer that you call me Henry."

"Henry." John sighed and gave in. "But it's still Mr. Hunter to you."

It was a lovely afternoon for walking, the second they had encountered in a row. The trees were mostly bare by now, which meant that despite the cold air, bright sun touched John's face, unfiltered by anything except a few branches reaching to the sky.

He'd left the sling behind several days ago. As he walked, he moved his arm, subtly, in its socket, testing the range—

just enough to twinge, a good kind of pain, before backing off.

Henry was talking.

That, John realized, would be surprising to nobody in the universe who knew the man at all.

Henry was amusing, thoughtful, a complete chatterbox, and—incidentally—also an inveterate liar. Percentage-wise he probably didn't lie much more than the average man. But given the sheer volume of words that proceeded from his mouth, he uttered approximately a hundred times more lies than John. And he had a tendency to deliver them all at once.

"So at any rate," Henry was saying, "when I was taking articles—"

"One moment." John held up a hand. "When you were taking articles? Isn't that what one does when one wants to be a barrister?"

Henry wrinkled his nose. "Ah. Yes. Well, so it is."

"Didn't you tell me once you were a potter's son?" Or maybe it had been a tailor. There had been as many professions as there had been days.

"Ah, ha ha. Well. Yes, I did, and there are potters' sons who… still, possibly that might have been a bit of a…um, how do I say this? A bit of an exaggeration." Henry gave him a brilliant smile. "My father…did own a pottery works? It wasn't entirely a lie."

More than two weeks of walking. Two weeks of Henry talking; several days of thinking of him as Henry rather than Latham, a transition that had occurred all too swiftly. That much time, John had spent listening to the other man's exaggerations. He was used to it by now.

"So your father owned a pottery works. You were planning to be a barrister. How did you wind up in the infantry?"

"Did you know that people want barristers who are capable of talking about the same thing for more than two minutes at a time?" Henry shot back brightly. "I *did* know that, but my father had to be convinced that it was the case."

"Your father the potter?"

"Uh. Yes. Him." Henry simply waved a hand. "It does all make sense, and I'll explain as soon as I...um, take care of some business over by that copse of trees. If you know what I mean."

John did know what he meant, and he wasn't referring to Henry's need to piss. Henry avoided all questions about his father, except to roundly decry him as terrible. The only thing John was sure of was that he *wasn't* a potter. He was likely not even a pottery works owner. Henry was hiding something.

It would be offensive, except he was so inept at hiding it hardly counted. It was like draping a blanket over a statue and pinning a sign to it that said *NO STATUE UNDER HERE, HA HA, WHY WOULD YOU THINK THAT?*

Henry's family was obviously wealthy—enough so that Henry, with his talk of equality and such, felt it an embarrassment.

But one could not hide the tracks left by wealth. John could hear it in his voice. He could hear it in his surprised exclamations.

"Who knew squirrel could be so delicious?" he'd remarked the first night they'd made stew of the hapless creatures who'd made the mistake of chattering excitedly at them from the road.

An officer in the infantry, and he'd never eaten squirrel? John knew that officers tended to use their own funds to purchase provisions, and that wealthy officers tended to eat well, but...

Never eaten *squirrel?*

He didn't complain about hard biscuit either. He acted as if it were a special treat.

"Goodness," Henry had said. "I'd always wondered what it was like, and now I know!"

He'd *wondered*. He had *wondered,* as if it were a line in a story and not the desperate reality for thousands of men.

Henry had just continued on the road, eating squirrels and hard biscuits with the absolutely terrible cheese that he tried every meal.

He may have been born wealthy, but his clumsy attempt to pretend otherwise was endearing. Or—at least—John corrected himself, it would have been, if John had been the sort to allow himself to be endeared. Henry hadn't even sighed wistfully five minutes ago when they'd passed a cottage. The wind had carried with it the scent of cooking food—savory meat and the yeasty smell of baking bread. Even John had glanced longingly in that direction before moving on.

It had been days since their last warm meal.

The wind shifted and John caught the scent of that bread again. He hoped Henry hurried his business up—story about his father or no, John hated wanting things he couldn't have, and bread was something of a personal weakness.

Crusty bread. Brown bread. Steaming bread, hot from the oven. Damn it.

John's stomach grumbled. At that moment, leaves crackled, presaging someone's arrival. He turned. Two men had come out of the trees. They were white, and they looked at John with narrowed eyes.

"Told you so," one said to the other.

"Walking about on the road, just like that."

God. The last thing John needed now was to be accosted by the locals. This, this was the sort of thing that might have happened to his mother in Newport. One day at the market, they might have—

He clamped down on that train of thought before it spread into panic.

"I'll be moving on," he assured them. "I've no desire to stay."

The two men exchanged glances. The one who spoke next had sandy-brown hair and a gap in his teeth. "But who knows what you've taken? That's what I say."

The other man—ruddy skin contrasting with dark, curly hair—nodded. "In fact," he said, "I think we should search your pack just to be sure you haven't stolen anything. We'll hold on to anything suspicious we find, just in case the real owners turn up."

So it was to be a kind of shakedown. He didn't have enough that he could afford to lose anything. John stepped in front of his pack. He was going to have to hold firm.

"Hand it over," said Gap Tooth.

John grimaced. "I would really rather not."

Curly Hair just shook his head. "It will be a real shame to have to report you to the constable. We live just down the road. He knows us." He pointed in the direction of the cottage. "We're good, God-fearing folk. *Who* knows *you?*"

"Oh dear Lord." The words came from behind them as Henry materialized from between the trees. "You mean you *don't* know him?"

They turned as one. They caught sight of Henry. He paused, as if on instinct, to let them look him over. There was no sign that he'd been doing his business. There was no sign that he'd been on the road for weeks. Every morning, he wielded his razor like an expert. His cheeks were close-shaven; his clothing was almost new. His boots were dark, the leather not cracked by time.

Henry held his own pack over his shoulder as if it were a light jacket instead of a bag containing all his worldly belongings. He posed, arm cocked at his hip, eyes bright and wide. He looked like he belonged anywhere—his glossy not-quite-blond hair, his too-jaunty hat, his coat that spoke of riches. He wasn't trying to look like a potter's son now.

The men frowned, then exchanged glances with each other. Those glances said that they had no idea what Henry was talking about.

John had been feeling that way for the last fortnight.

"You've truly never heard of him?" Henry asked. "That's Corporal John Hunter. Corporal. Jonathan. Lewis. Hunter. Does that jog your memory?"

John didn't have a middle name, but Henry said it so sincerely that he almost doubted his own memory.

Gap Tooth shook his head. "Not…really?"

Henry continued on. "Corporal Hunter, Scourge of the Rhode Island Regiment?" He waited expectantly. Curly Hair shrugged.

"John Hunter, Bane of the British? Ruin of the redcoats? Enemy of the English?"

The two men just squinted at Henry.

"Surely you have heard of the Lacerator of the Loyalists? The Curse of the Crown? *That* John Hunter?"

"Um." Gap Tooth looked as befuddled as John felt. "No?"

"For God's sake. I knew the British had suppressed news of our American heroes, but I didn't know they had been so successful. This is a travesty. An utter travesty."

Curly Hair's eyebrows scrunched down in confusion.

John had no idea what the other man was doing, but… Damn, this would not turn out well.

"Latham," John said through gritted teeth. "You're embarrassing me."

"Humble, too," Henry said, waving off the warning tone in John's voice. "Why, at the Battle of Germantown, he saved Washington himself from a detachment of British soldiers.

They had snuck into the encampment before him. Had you not *heard* this story of attempted assassination?"

"No!" Despite themselves, the two men crept closer to Latham.

"Yes!" Latham was clearly warming to his story. "Major General the Lord Cornwallis, God rot his soul, had the most dastardly plan. He intended to kill Washington by subterfuge, thus depriving the Continental Army of its most powerful leader."

Curly Hair gasped. "Of course he did, that worm."

"Cornwallis had his men slay seven Continental soldiers —good men, including my comrade Duncan—but that's a story for another day." Henry paused, looking upward, as if to commemorate the passing of a lost soul.

Curly Hair tilted his head.

"The threat to Washington? How'd that turn out?"

John found himself mildly curious about what he was supposed to have done, too.

"Ah." Henry seemed to return to the present. "That evil man dressed his most trusted, most stealthy soldiers in Continental blue. He sent them into the encampment where Washington was quartered. Washington had sent scouts out to survey the land. His aide-de-camp, the, uh…" Henry faltered. "The esteemed, uh—"

"Hamilton," John put in. "His name is Alexander Hamilton."

Henry waved a hand in his direction. "Don't interrupt me, Hunter. As I was saying. The esteemed Hamilton had gone to oversee the front. Never believe that Washington was left unprotected, of course; he was no fool. But those cowardly, cravenly men in American uniform strode into camp as if they owned the place. They walked through the encampment, and before anyone knew what was happening, they slew Washington's inner guard. Washington cried for help—but only one man had the eagle ears to hear it."

"Who was that?" John asked.

Henry gave him an annoyed look, quickly masked by a sweet smile. "I am *so* glad you asked. It was Jonathan Lewis Hunter, *that* was who. Just as the spying, lying British soldiers surrounded Washington, Hunter here" —Henry clapped John on the back—"entered his tent."

John glared at Henry; Henry looked at his hand and yanked his arm away with a sheepish smile.

"Gah," said Gap Tooth. "One man, against so many?"

"Precisely. John was just one man. He hadn't any warning. He had naught on him but…a stick." Henry looked off into the distance. "A stick and a single carving knife that he had been using to whittle it into a ship."

John raised an eyebrow.

"How was he to defend his commander with such an item?" Henry posed this hypothetical.

"General," John interjected. "Washington is a general."

"General," Henry conceded. He didn't look at John, just smiled at the other two men. "I used the word 'commander' to describe what he did—commanded. In other words, I used it generally. To encompass generals. But back to the matter at hand. Corporal Jonathan Lewis Hunter had only those sparse weapons, to compare with the muskets and the wicked swords of his seven enemies. But he had one thing they did not."

"What?" Curly Hair asked.

A man willing to lie for him? John knew better than to provide that answer.

"Determination. He looked those devils in the eye and said one thing: 'I cannot allow you to kill my commander.'"

That sounded like a great deal more than *one* thing. Still…

"General," John interjected.

"General," Henry agreed. "That's what I said, isn't it? Stop interrupting. 'I cannot allow you to kill my general,' he said. 'You'll get to him when you go through me.'"

"So what happened next?" Gap Tooth asked.

"What, next? Oh." Latham paused. He looked up at the sun and sighed. "I'm sorry, gentlemen. We haven't had a hot meal in days, and we mean to make South Brunswick by nightfall. We must be on our way."

Gap Tooth glanced at Curly Hair. Curly Hair looked back. The two men gave each other a nod.

"I'm William," said Gap Tooth. "William Williamson. This is my friend David Poitier."

"Williamson. Poitier." Latham nodded at them. "We're pleased to make your acquaintance. I'm just Henry Latham, but I hardly need to introduce my traveling companion. Jonathan Lewis Hunter himself."

The men glanced at Hunter.

"He may shake your hand if you ask nicely," Latham said. "But he's very circumspect. Too humble, really. He hates admitting his role in things."

Poitier and Williamson had apparently forgotten that they'd started the encounter by attempting to rob John. They glanced at each other. Then Williamson turned to John.

"Mr. Hunter," he said, holding out his hand, "it's truly an honor."

"I…" John sighed. He took the other man's hand. "Right."

Poitier elbowed Williamson, who coughed and spoke. "Would either of you…want some soup?"

CHAPTER SIX

They had soup—thick soup, laden with beef, barley, and carrots. There was bread, cut in generous slices and spread with butter.

There was, of course, the continuation of Henry's tale, which he was determined to render with as much animation as possible. It had, after all, earned them a dinner. He invented details. He was the *best* at inventing details. John defeated one man with a map pulled off a table, another with his own musket. He confounded a third by slinging buttons pulled off a fallen comrade into his eyes—"very effective weapons, buttons are, if hurled hard enough," Henry explained, and the two men nodded, drinking in every word as if the tale were as good as the soup.

Poitier cut up apples, listening with starry eyes, as Henry made his way through the ending.

"As our good corporal faced the last man," Henry said, "bodies strewn about him, blood streaming down his face, his knife held before him in a low grip, well, what do you think he said?"

Williams was watching, wide-eyed. "I don't know. What did he say?"

"'You'll get to my general when you get through me.'" Henry gave a low growl. "He had no thought of his own wounds. He thought only of Washington, our great American Republic, and freedom. He raised his knife."

Henry gestured with his hands—one raised like the blade he'd described, the other gesturing an unknown assailant forward.

"What heroism!" Poitier clasped his hands together.

Beside him, Hunter rolled his eyes. "It was nothing," he said in a tone that conveyed that it had, in fact, been literally nothing.

Henry ignored that shameful failure to play along. "Faced with such courage, there was nothing the enemy could do. The man dropped his sword and ran, a coward to the end."

Poitier cheered. "Good riddance to the British bastard!"

Henry nodded solemnly. He was himself a British bastard; he ought to get some small satisfaction playing the role. "General Washington himself gave me the sacred command to accompany Hunter home. Loyalists still speak his name in hushed, envenomed whispers. Washington feared for his safety on the road. So here I am. And, gentlemen, we thank you for the meal—but we must be on our way."

Williamson sighed, as if he didn't wish to come to his senses. Poitier looked as if he'd been struck with a bouquet of daisies, a silly smile playing all over his face.

"Take some biscuits," Poitier said. "You'll be hungry come evening. It's the least we can do for such a hero."

"I'll wrap some roast chicken," Williamson offered.

"And the apples. We've an abundance of apples; we'll be sick of apples by midwinter."

They returned to the road fifteen minutes later, laden with fruit, nuts, and wax paper packets of chicken.

There was a feeling of exuberance that Henry got when he managed to make others happy. He felt it now. It put a lightness in his step, got him to whistling. Why, when he'd first encountered those men, they had been…

Um.

Too late, he realized that they'd been incredibly hostile to Hunter. So hostile. Good God, he'd forgotten about that, getting carried away with his story. He'd intervened, not thinking of anything except lightening the mood. And then… He had gotten a little carried away. They'd lost an hour's walking time.

"So." He glanced over at Hunter. "Well. About that…story. I'm sure…you're wondering where it came from."

Hunter looked over at him. His face was an unreadable mask. "A stick. A knife. That's what I fought seven men off with?"

"There were buttons," Henry protested. "Do not forget the buttons."

"Did you know those two intended to rob me before you appeared?"

"Indeed. I panicked, not remembering any Latin."

Hunter was probably angry. He had every reason to be. The two of them had even been talking about Henry's lies when he'd wandered off. Now the man must think him an even bigger liar.

And he wasn't *wrong*.

"I suppose…" Henry bit his lip. "Maybe… I shouldn't have…"

John broke and snickered. He actually *snickered*. "No, please don't apologize."

Henry stared at the other man a moment.

"You're not…angry?"

"That was the most ridiculous thing I've *ever* seen. You just...you told them that I—and a *stick*—" Another round of guffaws shook his shoulders.

"I got slightly carried away," Henry admitted. "I don't know why I do this—these ideas just pop into my head and I say them without thinking. I can't even blame my upbringing. My father did his best to make me stop, but..."

"But people like listening to you talk," Hunter said, "and so he never managed to make the lesson stick."

Henry blinked. He looked over at Hunter. "Did you just say...?"

"Of *course* people like listening to you talk." Hunter repeated that as if it were obvious. "You're funny, and even when you're lying you say things that people want to believe. You're not frivolous, no matter what you've been told. You mean well and you like people, and you make them want to like you in return. Anyone who mistakes that for frivolity has no understanding of human nature."

Henry stopped walking. A brown bird flew overhead. The sky was clear and the air frigid. Reality seemed very close all of a sudden.

Hunter realized he'd stopped a few moments later. He turned, raised one eyebrow inquiringly. "What? If you're going to stop dead in your tracks every time I say something vaguely positive about you, this will be a very long journey. Hurry up now."

The implication that there would be *more*... Henry hastened to catch up, his head spinning.

"What?" Hunter asked. "Surely you've *noticed* that people like you by now?"

It had never been put to him in those terms. *People like you.* It was such a radical departure from the image he had in his own head—*talks too much, barely tolerated*—that for a second, he could not accommodate both thoughts. They warred in his head.

Nobody wants to listen to you.

Just thinking that it might not be true made Henry want to babble all the more.

"It's not that," Henry finally said, struggling to mask his feelings. "It's—it's amazing, I suppose, that instead of saying, 'Well, Henry, I think you're a decent fellow,' you have to hide behind general talk of *people* and such-like. Admit it. You like me."

"People like you." Hunter shrugged. "I generally count myself as a person. Where is the problem?"

"You admit it, then. You don't hate me!"

Hunter just smiled. "If I did, I'd have killed you outside Philadelphia. I've been known to take on an entire British regiment with a stick and a paring knife. You'd go down, no trouble at all."

Their eyes met. It was such a foolish thing, to be so happy that someone was issuing threats in his direction, but they weren't threats, and it was so lovely, so lovely. After a moment, they both laughed.

Oh, Henry thought, oh. This was nice. This was very nice. He could get used to this. He could get used to this, even though he knew he shouldn't.

"Hunter," he said, "I'll remind you that you said that later. No trouble at all. It sounds not very like me, doesn't it?"

Hunter just looked at him and shook his head. "Oh for God's sake."

"Mmm?"

"Call me John."

～

"Here." It was night. They'd made camp, and a small fire to warm their hands over. Henry leaned across the stone that sat between them, handing John something. "I'm not taking no for an answer again. Try it."

He dropped the slice of cheese into John's waiting palm. His fingertips touched John's hand briefly—a hint of warmth, quickly disappearing into the cold of night.

Henry cut off his own bit of cheese. The odor was rank this close, pungent and foul.

"Has it got any better?" John wrinkled his nose, inspecting the cheese.

"Not yet, but it should start improving any day now."

"You want me to voluntarily put this in my mouth and eat it?"

"Yes, and furthermore, while you do, say to yourself: 'The cheese is delicious.'"

John's eyes met Henry's. A spark from the fire popped, burning orange between them before going dark.

"'The cheese is delicious.'"

"Not in that monotone. Say it like you mean it. 'This *cheese* is *delicious*.' There. Like that."

John's voice lowered to something almost smoky. "This cheese is *delicious*."

Henry felt that last word inside him, like a caress.

"There." John brought his hand to his mouth.

Henry did likewise. It would have been almost romantic —looking into each other's eyes, raising their hands simultaneously to their lips.

It would have been romantic, except the taste of death hit his tongue, dissolving into a thousand liquid deaths.

The cheese was most decidedly *not* delicious.

Across from him, John coughed. He sputtered.

"Oh fuck me," John said, spitting the cheese out. "No warning! You gave me absolutely no warning."

Henry laughed through his mouthful. "I did! I told you it was terrible every night!"

"I knew it was bad—you said it was bad—this cheese is not *bad*."

The main objective in the moment, Henry realized, was to not snort grains of foul-tasting cheese out of his nose. He clamped his hands over his mouth.

"*Bad* is for things that are ordinarily bad. *Armies* would unite to fight this cheese. This is the cheese of hell."

Henry swallowed his own cheese. "The cheese is delicious," he managed to choke out. "My...taste in cheese? May need some time to, um, become accustomed to that fact."

John pointed a finger at him over the fire. "That is not how reality works," he warned. "You cannot change reality just by insisting it's not so. That's called delusion, not reality."

"You're probably right. But—for the sake of argument—what if we were born deluded, and had to be, um, undeluded? I imagine it would take time."

"No amount of time would change the Cheese of Death into anything other than the Cheese of Death."

"Care to place a bet?"

"What stakes could possibly justify *that*? I'd have to eat the cheese. *Often*."

Henry frowned. "Loser must provide the winner with a medal proclaiming 'Well, at least you tried.'"

Their eyes met across the fire. Henry waggled one eyebrow in what he hoped was a winning manner. And apparently, it worked.

"Well." John's lips twitched into a crooked smile. "Who wouldn't risk certain death for such a prize?"

~

"To you," John said, lifting his cheese like a libation of hard spirits about thirty miles from the Connecticut border. "The cheese is delicious."

Henry ate his own cheese. "A fine bouquet," he said, still choking on the taste. "There's…an underlying flavor, if you pay attention."

"Beneath the taste of death mold."

"Yes, beneath that."

"Once you ignore the feeling of impending doom that takes over your taste buds."

"Yes, definitely ignore that. There's an underlying subtleness that is almost…not completely terrible."

"Not completely terrible," John said. "You *are* making strides."

"Do you see what I mean? That…subtle…thing there, at the end? Surely you taste it."

"No," John replied. "It's all terrible."

"Speaking of not completely terrible," Henry said, two nights later after they'd performed their usual ritual of cheese eating and cheese complaining, "if you think Jefferson is so awful, how is it you were fighting with the Continental forces?"

John looked at him over the fire. Slowly, he sighed.

"You had to have *some* feeling for this…America…thing." He could not believe it had not occurred to him before.

John's eyes shut. "I wasn't fighting for the Revolution. I was fighting for Lizzie. And Noah."

Henry waited.

"When I was sixteen," John said, "my master hit hard

times. Mostly self-inflicted—gambling was always his issue. He sold my mother."

John said that so matter-of-factly, yet at his side, his hand clenched.

"Up until that point, I had only dreamed of running away. I'd made elaborate plans. I knew when I'd leave. What I would say beforehand to allay suspicion. I even knew what to do to guarantee my freedom so long as I made it far enough. But…"

"You needed a push?"

"But there was my mother. And Lizzie, my little sister? I had told myself a pack of lies—that I could protect her, that I could make our master listen. She was his child. I thought that meant *something*, that one day, as long as I made myself useful…" John shrugged this away. "It was a delusion, and I lost my delusions. At the end of the day, he sold my mother, and my delusions were no comfort at all. So I left."

"As you should have."

John's hand clenched at his side. "I left Lizzie. She was too little to come, too little to even trust. I couldn't tell her I was going; if there was any chance she would spill my secrets, it would ruin everything. I left her there, in slavery, all alone, at eleven—no mother, no brother, no protection." His voice trembled. "Anything could have happened to her."

"Did it?"

John exhaled a long breath. His hands unclenched. "No. I made my way north. I found a job, I learned to read. I changed my last name to Hunter—it sounded strong, and the name he had given me did not seem like one I wanted to keep." A faint smile touched his lips. "I knew my master had been cheating his business partner, and that plan I had for freedom? When I left, I took his account books. Once I had a firm foothold in life, I found someone trustworthy to go to him and tell him that if he didn't release me and my sister and give us paperwork that declared us freed, I'd send his partner his account books."

"Did that work?"

"It did." John sighed. "My mother—finding her, raising the money to free her, that took another five years. But Lizzie came of age a free woman in Rhode Island, and..." John's smile was just a little sad.

"And?"

"She fell in love. His name was Noah Allan, and he was enslaved."

"In Rhode Island? I thought slavery was a Southern practice."

The fire flickered across John's face, illuminating those perfect cheekbones. He was looking away, at something.

"Mmm. Not so much. There are more than a handful of slaves in Rhode Island. As for Newport itself... It depends heavily on the slave trade. Or at least it did, before the British occupied it. I told Lizzie to love someone else, but... Well, apparently love doesn't work like that."

No, Henry thought stupidly, watching the fire play across John's skin. It didn't.

"We had plans for him, too. It was going to take time and saving. But then war broke out, and Mr. Allan's son enlisted, full of patriotic fervor. Some time later, Rhode Island announced that any slave who enlisted would be automatically freed. Noah was all set to enlist. Newport was occupied at the time, but it would have been no large matter for a slave to slip out in order to pass muster. But Mr. Allan cried that he needed the help, and Lizzie just cried, and..." John shrugged. "And I thought Lizzie had had enough of men she loved leaving her to obtain their freedom. So I made a contract with Mr. Allan. I'd enlist in Noah's stead, and in exchange he agreed to free him when the war ended, or upon my death, or after three years."

There was a way that John said Lizzie's name, something both soft and impenetrable, all at once. "You fought in a war you didn't believe in for *years* to free the man your sister loved?"

John shrugged, as if it were nothing. "People have fought wars for far stupider reasons. And this time I told her why I was going, and I promised to come back to her."

"And here you are. Coming back."

John looked away. "It was a lie," he said softly. "Every man who died on a battlefield had promised some sweetheart he would return. Some months ago, Allan freed Noah. He and Lizzie were married, and there began to be...incidents. Newport was much worsened by the British occupation, and people who have little often resent those they believe should have less. Rudenesses at first, then things left on my family's doorstep. My sister said she expected they'd be warned out at any moment."

"People are terrible."

"I promised to come back," John said softly, "and here I am, coming, as fast as I can. But I have not heard from Lizzie in six months, and I do not know if there is a back to return to any longer."

Henry swallowed. "I'm sure—"

John held up a hand. "You're not sure of anything. I'll say it all for you. The mail in the army has been wretched. It was wretched during the occupation, and it's not much better now. I try not to let the worry wear down my spirit, but..." Another shrug. "If I've been a bit harsh with you, that's why. I've been eaten up with worry these last weeks."

Henry sat up straight, started to reach out a hand, and then pulled it back. "Don't apologize."

Their eyes met again over the fire. A spark blossomed in his chest, painful and fierce and desperate, all at once. It was a wild feeling. A generous feeling. He wanted to take the world down, brick by brick, and put it back together again the way it was supposed to be. Nobody should have to worry, not like this. Least of all John.

Oh, Henry thought. *Oh. That's what this is.* It was… Friendship, but warmer. Care, but with a softness to it. It was a journey shared, coming closer to the end with every day.

"Very well," John said. "Then I won't apologize. You'll do it prettily enough for both of us if I just keep my mouth shut."

"*You* made a joke." Henry found himself smiling. "I like when you make jokes."

John didn't smile in response. That would have trivialized the light in his eyes, the amused purse of his lips. He didn't smile, but he shook his head. "I do that sometimes. That's what friends do."

CHAPTER SEVEN

J ohn eyed that night's cheese dubiously. It had become a ritual between them—cheese every night, just before dinner, so they could drown out the taste with whatever meal they had.

The fire was crackling; the brace of pigeons he'd fetched with his sling roasted merrily on a spit. When he stretched his arm, he could almost straighten it all the way out before his shoulder complained. He could mark the passing of this journey by these little things.

"The cheese is delicious," he said.

"Say it as if you mean it, John." Henry spoke from across the fire.

John looked up. Looked into his companion's eyes—wide, open, inviting.

"The cheese is *delicious*."

Speaking of things they were lying about...He didn't know why he did it—maybe for no better reason than it made him happy in a way that was deeply selfish—but he always tried to make eye contact with Henry when he said those words. He emphasized the word delicious, rolling the syllables off his tongue.

Delicious.

Henry flushed, right on cue. And if John's own cheeks heated, well, that was no business of anyone's but his. Henry would never detect the blush.

John wasn't sure when Henry had transformed from *pretty British officer, not to be trusted* into *friend, definitely should be teased*. He wasn't sure if he was teasing himself or Henry. Both, he suspected.

That low sense of awareness built between them, coiling in John's gut, buzzing just beneath his skin. It simmered at night when they lay back-to-back.

But Henry hadn't said a word about it, for all his blushes, and if *Henry* didn't want to have a conversation about a topic, there was probably a reason. When Henry wanted to talk about his attraction to men in general, and John in particular, John trusted that he would do so. At length.

"Well?" That faint pinkening of Henry's cheeks—his entire face, nose, forehead—deepened under John's perusal. "If the cheese is delicious, eat it."

John put it in his mouth.

Maybe it was because he was still watching Henry. Maybe it was because he was thinking about Henry's attraction to him and avoiding the more salient, pressing matter of his own attraction to Henry. Maybe it was just the cheese.

Whatever the reason might have been, John's life changed forever in that moment for one undeniable reason.

He forgot to hate the cheese.

He forgot it so thoroughly, looking into Henry's eyes, that he didn't cough. He didn't spit out his mouthful. He chewed. He swallowed.

"My God," Henry murmured worshipfully. "It's happening. It's finally happening. I *told* you it was happening."

"What's happening?"

"I *told* you," Henry cackled. "I told you that it was starting to change. I told you that there was a richness to the flavor, but did you listen? No."

Oh. God. Damn. John straightened where he sat, tasting the lingering flavor on his tongue with something close to horror. It *had* been bad, hadn't it? Wretched? Disgusting?

"It wasn't *good*," he said defensively. "Don't get me wrong. There was nothing *good* about it. Contempt for the Cheese of Death has wrought familiarity, that's all."

"Just wait. I've been doing this longer than you. This is how it starts."

This was how it started—watching the play of fire over Henry's skin, the shift of his smiles. This was how it started, treasuring the flash of his eyes, the ripple of the muscles in his behind when he stood and bent over the fire, poking the pigeons, sending a few drops of their juice to land sizzling in the coals.

It had started with teasing and friendship, and John had no idea where it would go.

John just shook his head. "This is how it *ends*."

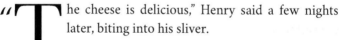

"The cheese is delicious," Henry said a few nights later, biting into his sliver.

It wasn't delicious, not at the moment. But it had gone from utterly disgusting to almost palatable, and at this rate of progression, it would likely be ambrosia by the end of the year.

"The cheese is delicious," John echoed, sliding his own bite into his mouth. His tongue was shockingly pink, the cheese a white morsel against his skin. His skin drank up the firelight, reflecting orange and red and pink. Henry wanted to chase the sight of those colors with his fingers, tracing them, warm, along the path up John's neck. He shouldn't think of John's lips, but he did.

Also, he didn't think John *minded* him thinking of his lips, as he hadn't said anything like *why are you staring at my lips?* John would definitely have said that if he objected.

Possibly not.

"God rot it," John said in annoyance, frowning up at the starry firmament. "The cheese is improving. We can't have this."

"It's only natural."

"It is *not*. This should not work. You can't change the world around you just by claiming it's different."

"Of course you can," Henry said. "Once upon a time, somebody said 'Look, this piece of paper here equals a bit of gold,' and then everyone agreed that it was and here we are."

"Well, that's—"

"And once upon a time, someone stuck a bunch of sticks in the ground and said 'All the stuff inside these sticks is mine,' and everyone else said, 'Right-o' and went to fetch their own sticks. Most of the things we believe to be true are only true because we believe them, instead of the reverse."

"So if I believed you to be a rabbit…" John smiled at him.

"Ah, me!" Henry brightened. "My favorite topic of conversation. As it turns out, I am an *excellent* example of this phenomenon. You see, my father always believed me a frivolous man."

"Incapable of seeing beyond his nose, more like," John muttered.

"And so did everyone around him," Henry said. "Was he wrong? Or was his belief so powerful that he rendered me frivolous?"

"The fact that you can consider so ridiculous a question

without bursting into laughter at the nonsensical nature of it rather agitates for the conclusion that you are not frivolous."

"My father told me, when he purchased my commission, that he hoped I died valiantly in battle, as it would be the only way I could do credit to the family."

John lifted the lid off the pot on the fire and poked at something inside it. "Your father is the anti-cheese. On inspection, he grows worse and worse."

"And then I arrived here," Henry said, "and I read that circular, and I had my thoughts. I engaged in the most frivolous treason anyone has ever engaged in. Even with him half an ocean distant, I couldn't undo his beliefs, though. I had made my peace with dying because he believed I should. It's hard to explain, but… I felt my choice was between living in England, frivolous and stupid, or dying here with a brain in my head. I couldn't imagine any other alternative."

"And now?"

"Now?" Henry sighed. "I'm living in a dream. In my dream, I'm on a journey. It's a place removed from reality, and so I'm able to believe whatever I like."

"Yes," John said with a snort, "now *there* I very much disagree. I am not some figment of your dream. I exist. I am real. This is life, not some walking nightmare."

"For you it is," Henry said, eyes meeting his. "At the end of this journey, you'll have family and a home there to greet you."

John glanced sharply away.

"You told me to walk away from my life and not go back, but…" Henry sighed. "It's not practical. I have no skills except cheesemongering, and even that is suspect, as it takes any person weeks to find my cheese passable. Also, we are on the way to running out."

John did not point out that a potter's son ought to have had some skills. He didn't ask where the officers' commission had come from. With the exception of a few tiny comments, he let Henry's falsehoods lie when he could have made much of them. Henry was grateful for that. Still…

"I have sisters who are no doubt worrying about me, and a mother who is weeping, and even my terrible father may yet regret advising me to perish in a blaze of glory. I don't want to be a frivolous, irresponsible fellow, but walking away from the British Army in a fit of pique in the middle of battle may be the most frivolous thing I've ever done." Henry looked at John. "I don't want to die, but I don't know how to *live*, either."

John didn't say anything. He just stood, moved to sit next to Henry on the log. Having John close, having him sit down, his thigh warmed by the fire next to Henry—it was too much.

"And here you are," Henry said, "being kind to me when you have so many more non-frivolous things to worry about, and I'm spilling this *rubbish* on your shoulders."

John just took his hand. His fingers traced a pattern on Henry's palm. "Well, you know I can't outtalk you."

Henry's breath stopped. John was touching him. After weeks of distance, weeks of keeping a few careful inches between their backs at night… His mind ceased to function. He could feel his whole body shut down in appreciation. He looked blindly up at John, and even though his entire being was being consumed, he found he could still talk, because of course he could. "Nobody can outtalk me. It's a fact of nature."

"I don't know how to tell you to live. I rather think that's something you'll have to figure out for yourself."

His fingers traced a vein up Henry's arm, and oh, Henry wanted. He wanted to curl his fingers around John's wrist in return. He wanted to *live*.

"Yes, but—"

"But if I had made this trip alone, I'd have spent the entire time worrying myself into nothingness. I'd have had no conversation, nobody to make me laugh, nobody to feed me cheese, nobody to make me think."

"Nobody to save you from bandits with ridiculous stories," Henry said.

John reached out. The tips of his fingers brushed Henry's face, and Henry felt his heart stop.

Oh, God. If he believed his heart was stopping now, would he actually be dead? Was it possible to perish from a sharp influx of pleasure? Could one pass away from delight?

Henry took a breath, then another.

Apparently one couldn't, because John was touching him, and Henry had not died. That slow caress continued down his cheek.

"I don't know what to say to you except this," John murmured. "You have not been frivolous to me. You have been the foundation on which this journey is built. You have been necessary."

"Necessary?" Henry echoed.

John's thumb touched his lips.

"Necessary," John repeated.

Henry exhaled. He set his hand over John's. He should say something—anything. He didn't.

"When you figure out how to live again," John said, and he uttered *when* as if it were a foregone conclusion, not *if*, and Henry wanted, wanted, wanted, wanted to believe that *when* with his entire body. He wanted that *when* from the tips of his fingers, brushing against John's hand, to the thud of his heart. He wanted it from the aroused tingle that traveled down his spine all the way to his still-silent lips. "When you figure it out, then let me know."

Like smoke, John's hand slipped away.

~

For some reason—a haze of lust, perhaps, or inexplicable happiness, or some combination of the two—Henry found himself babbling throughout the next day.

No topic was too stupid for him not to remark upon. Chicken sexing (a noble career, although impossible to do, which Henry knew because he had tried when he was seven to no avail). Dogfighting (an ignoble career). Familial infighting (not a career, all too easy to do, but never as satisfying in reality as imagining a far superior outcome to the conversation in one's head).

He talked about everything except the one thing on his mind. Or perhaps it was not on his mind. Perhaps it was on his cock. In his cock? The particulars escaped him. How had they managed to *not* talk about this one thing over the course of their journey?

Henry had talked of literally everything else under the sun; why not this?

It wasn't that the topic was taboo.

Well. So. It was, technically, but that had never stopped Henry.

It wasn't as if he feared that John would fly into a rage or express disgust. They'd practically kissed last night.

Maybe it was simply that they had not talked about this one thing yet, despite its glaring obviousness, and it had now become awkward.

That awkwardness grew from morning to noon, from noon to late afternoon. By the time they were setting up camp that evening, the awkwardness—at least the awkwardness in Henry's mind—had grown to epic proportions.

So Henry did what he often did with awkward situations.

He blurted out precisely what was on his mind, just as they were unrolling their blankets.

"So," he heard himself say, "I know I've never mentioned this before, but I'm certain you realize that I've fucked men?"

John's face went utterly blank for one heart-stopping second. Then he laughed. "Oh, God. Henry. Only *you*. Only you would announce it in that fashion."

Henry felt his face heat.

"No," John said, "I did *not* know that, not for certain."

"How could you not know? Was I insufficiently obvious?"

"Well." John considered that. "You were very obvious. But that only told me that you admired men the way I do."

Well. Good. They were both speaking about it.

"But I could hardly conclude anything about past behavior," John said.

Why *had* they not spoken of it when it was so easy? Apparently that was all that needed to be said to make it not awkward any longer. Henry laid his sleeping roll out, then fetched water while John skinned the rabbit he'd snared that morning.

They made the fire together. Henry clipped wizened bits of carrot and turnip into the stew pot while John broke down the rabbit carcass.

He peered into his pack, rummaged around, before sitting up with a frown. "We're out of bread."

"Ah well," John said. "We'll live."

They would. They'd done so before. But Henry liked bread, and he knew that John regarded him as just a little soft in comparison. He bit his lip. "There's a household not a mile back. I could pay for a loaf, I'd wager."

"We're both exhausted. Rest; we need to make our miles tomorrow."

"But John…" Henry tried to think of his very best argument. "*Bread*."

"Oh, you think I'll give in if you bat your eyelashes prettily? Well, it's your coin and your feet. But you could stay here and tell me more about the fact you've fucked men."

"You're *teasing* me."

"Yes, and you don't dislike it. Did your father know? Did he do anything terrible to you?"

How John got to the heart of the matter so swiftly, Henry would never know.

"Here I am." Henry gestured expansively. "Sent into the army to atone for my terrible sins, preferably by dying valiantly."

John brought one hand up to his mouth as if to hide a smile.

"What? It's actually not funny. He was most insistent. He said awful things."

"I'm sure he did." John bit his lip, his eyes dancing. "I'm sure he was thinking, 'Oh, no, the *infantry*, that will definitely solve everything.'"

"He did!" Henry said. "How did you know? He said almost exactly those words!"

"I'm sure he said to your mother something like this: 'Dear, our Henry likes to fuck men, so let's surround him with men, preferably fit ones used to a march. Make sure they're dressed in tight trousers and sharp uniforms.'"

"There you veer off from reality. I am certain he did not say that."

"'Let's make him an officer. It will be his *duty* to watch them march. Let's surround him with *men all the time.*'"

"I see what you're getting at," Henry said, "and I believe he was thinking of military discipline."

"And did that stop you from fucking men?"

"Well—no."

"You and half the infantry, I'd wager. Henry, I hate to tell you this, but your father? I am going to guess he's something of a fool." John laughed. "He sent you into the infantry to teach you proper behavior?"

"Almost his exact words! In his defense," Henry said, "he'd never joined. How would he know?"

John laughed harder.

"And in his defense," Henry said, "I *have* become more circumspect. I'm much better at judging who is safe to talk to." He threw that out, holding his breath.

John looked over at him. "'Talk.' Is that how fancy British officers describe fucking?"

Henry's heart hammered in his chest. He looked John in the eyes. "What do you call it?"

John stirred the stew and shrugged.

"I've never had a commission bought for me. I've no choice but to be circumspect. I don't call it anything."

Henry exhaled slowly.

"I just do it," John said on a hoarse whisper.

Not a whisper. An invitation.

Their eyes met again. Henry felt a tug of energy go through him. In an ideal world, Henry would have intuited the perfect thing to say, something sweet and romantic, something that matched the growing lightness in his soul. He'd have said something that somehow captured the inchoate feelings that John aroused in him, and they'd have fallen—very slowly, very romantically—into a conveniently placed bower of petals.

Henry had never said the perfect thing in his life, and besides, it was almost winter and the closest they'd get to a bower of petals would be a pile of moldering leaves. With the wind whipping around them, even that was absent.

So what Henry said was this: "You must have done a great deal. You're so very pretty."

John's eyes widened. "Nobody has ever called me pretty before."

"No? Whyever not?"

"It's just not...done, I suppose."

"And now it has been done, and should be done a thousand times over. You're very pretty, you know. And intelligent. And—" He bit off a thousand other adjectives that came to mind. "If it were spring, I'd make you a daisy crown and prove it. But you have lovely, mobile, expressive eyes and a strong chin and a sharp jawline, and..."

And, oh, God, where was that bower of petals! He wanted to hide his face in it. His whole body, in fact. He'd just said, aloud, that John was pretty, in a tone that let all his more flowery sentiments show.

It was a pity there was no bower of petals. Henry could crawl inside and perish of shame. Hell, he'd settle for hiding in that pile of debris.

"Henry," John said easily, "you eat terrible cheese and think that Thomas Jefferson has good qualities. You'll excuse me if I find you lacking in good taste."

Ouch. John said it with a smile on his face, but it hurt. It hurt with an almost painful intensity. It hurt as if John were extending an invitation for just a fuck and no more, after all their weeks together. He'd had relations that meant no more, but this—

Henry stood. "You couldn't be more correct. I am an utter idiot. I should never have said any such thing."

John looked at him.

"I should have said," Henry said, "that you were devastatingly beautiful."

John still didn't say anything.

"But then, I have no taste," Henry said. "Me and my terrible taste, we're going to get bread."

"Henry."

"Good thing you're used to swill," Henry muttered. "Who

knows what I'll come back with? After all, I have no good taste."

~

I t took about ten minutes of disconsolately stirring soup for John's sour mood to fade, and for him to recognize the truth: He'd made a mistake. He knew how Henry longed for acceptance, and his words had been hurtful. However he might try to justify his sentiments, it was not right, nor was it fair, to treat Henry as he had.

Compliments... They made him uneasy. They always made him feel as if someone was trying to get something from him. And while Henry obviously wanted things from him, those things were mutual and pleasurable and not to be argued over.

John was in the process of constructing an apology when the dust from the road presaged Henry's return.

Henry, I was unfair.

Henry, I'm so deeply sorry that I hurt you.

Henry, I never want to see you with that hurt in your eyes again.

Henry turned off the road and came up to their camp under the trees. John *had* to get this right.

Oh, damn it. Henry had become important to him. He cared what Henry thought, felt a stab of pain in his own heart when he saw the hurt reflected in the other man's eyes.

"Oi, John!" Henry called as he approached, waving madly. "You'll never guess what happened!"

Oh, *no*. John was glad to see him. So glad that his heart lifted. They were less than a hundred miles from their destination. How dreadfully inconvenient.

"Let me guess," John said dryly. "Your traveling

93

companion was an unconscionable ass, and you've obtained a cold shoulder to give to him."

Henry blinked at him. His lips compressed.

For a moment, he tilted his head in confusion. Then he laughed. "Oh, ha! I'd forgotten completely! I was annoyed at you for ten entire minutes, John!"

"Good God! Ten *entire* minutes."

"I know!" Henry set down the sack he'd slung over his shoulder and took out a loaf of bread, some radishes, and a bunch of carrots.

"Ten minutes on just one topic," he said, slicing bread. "How utterly single-minded of me. But then I got distracted! *Guess* what distracted me."

"Ah…"

"No, don't guess, it will take too long and I have no patience. I'm just going to tell you. It was cheese. That farmwife up there makes her own cheese."

"We have so much cheese. Why would you *buy* cheese?"

"First, we're running out. We do *not* have so much cheese. Second, I mean actual cheese. *Tasty* cheese. Cheese that one likes to eat. We don't have any of that. I was going to buy a small portion just for myself, so I could taunt you by saying you didn't want any of my cheese since I have no taste."

"Fitting punishment."

"But something happened. I tasted her cheese and…it didn't taste right."

"It wasn't good?"

"No. I'm afraid…" Henry swallowed. "I must confess. I'm very afraid that it *was* good. Objectively speaking."

"Oh," John breathed. "Oh, *no*."

"Oh, *yes*."

"John. It has *happened*. My tastes have become objectively *terrible*. You were completely right." He unwrapped the Cheese of Death and cut off a slice. He popped it in his mouth and chewed morosely. "I'm doomed. I like it. I actually like it."

"You should still be angry at me."

"Hush, I don't want to be. It's no fun."

"I shouldn't snap at you when you compliment me. That was terrible. I'm sorry."

"Well, then, boo." Henry wagged his fingers at him. "Consider yourself chastised. Want some cheese?"

"Henry. I'm trying to be serious."

"I am too. I realized it on my walk home. I ought to have been beaten to death for my mouth long before now. I'm scarcely tolerable as a white man, and people have been *trained* to tolerate me."

"Stop talking about yourself that way," John said. "Stop saying you don't deserve respect or care, because you do. It's not acceptable to me for anyone to dismiss you that way. Not at all. I'll fight anyone who says otherwise, especially when it's me."

Henry looked over at him. Their eyes caught, held. There was something—something bright and yet inexplicable in Henry's face.

"Oh," Henry said. "I wonder when that happened."

"When did what happen?"

"When did your good opinion become so utterly necessary to me?"

"I..." John trailed off. There was that word between them again. *Necessary.* It felt so much heavier than all the other words—lust, want, care, attention. It didn't fit, it couldn't fit, not with Newport so close. But Henry kept going.

"I feel pity for my former self, not knowing you at all. I can't garner a single ounce of regret for my childhood felonies any longer."

"What?" John pulled back. "*Felonies*? How did we get to felonies?"

"I was sixteen when I committed my first executable felony, you know. Buggery."

"Ah, that." John waved a hand as if batting a fly. "That's hardly even a felony. Henry, we were talking about—"

"Treason is my *second* felony. Being a hardened criminal dedicated to tearing down all the old institutions rather agrees with me, don't you think?"

There was nothing to do but give up and wait for the conversation to take them back to where they'd been. John tried to lead it there. He looked at Henry and said in his lowest, most sensual voice: "Felony looks good on you."

"Oh." Henry flushed. "I like it when you say it like that. Maybe I should add sedition to my list. My father will be so... What's the opposite of proud?"

"Annoyed? Dismayed? Outraged?"

"It will be glorious." Henry set his hand atop John's. The weight burned into him. "Let me lead you into a life of crime."

"Lead me? You can't lead me. I'm well ahead of you."

"Never! I cannot admit it. Name your crimes, sir. I *must* be the more dastardly."

"Aiding a runaway slave. Running away myself. Aiding another runaway slave. Fraud, blackmail in obtaining papers for my mother and sister." John shrugged. "The ever-present buggery."

Henry leaned in admiringly. "Damn you. You're right. You win. What excellent felonies. The *best* felonies. I have set my sights entirely too low! I need to break more laws."

"Ah." John smiled. "I've been an even worse influence than Thomas Jefferson, I see."

"What are friends for, if not to urge you on in the commission of crimes required by all men of moral character?"

Here was the tug he could give the conversation. John

leaned in until he could see nothing but Henry's smile, the freckles on his nose. "Is it friends, then, that we are?" Their breath danced on each other's lips, warm and perfect.

Henry pulled away. "Here," Henry said in the way he had that suggested he was speaking in perfect non sequiturs—or maybe not. "Have some dreadful cheese. It's still objectively terrible."

He cut a slice.

Oh, what the hell. John didn't take the cheese from Henry's hand. He leaned forward and took it in his mouth, letting his lips brush Henry's fingers.

He knew what to expect. He'd eaten the cheese often enough.

There was a burst of salt on his tongue, then a deep, rich flavor. Something that filled his mouth with an astonishing intensity.

And beneath that, there were layers—something sweet, something bitter, something sharp, coming together with a complexity that made absolutely no sense at all but formed an almost perfect balance...

"Oh no," John said. "It's happened."

"Has it?"

"How?" John pulled away. "How is this possible? How can this happen? How did the Cheese of Death turn into...this? What did you do? What were you thinking?"

"I was really thinking," Henry said, "that if you were going to kiss me, we had better both taste of cheese. But I can explain. It's simple. We hold these truths to be self-evident, that...all cheese is created equal."

"You are the most impossible man to try to kiss."

Henry just grinned at him.

"That when any form of cheesemongering becomes destructive of these ends, it is the right of the people to abolish it—"

"Do *not* continue, Henry. By no means are you to do this."

"*Make* me stop." Henry's eyes twinkled. "Where was I? Ah. It is the right of the people to abolish it and to institute new cheesemongers—"

In the end, there was only one way to shut him up.

CHAPTER EIGHT

Henry couldn't remember the last time he'd laughed so hard. "It is the right of the people to abolish and institute new cheesemongers," he managed to sputter out between guffaws, and he was about to go on when John set a finger across his lips.

"Mmm?"

John leaned in. He set the back of his other hand against Henry's cheek. "Henry," he said on a low murmur. "Henry."

"I know. You don't need to tell me. I'm being an idiot."

The finger on his lips pushed in. "No," John said. "You're quick, and you're funny, and you're clever, and you don't stop thinking about a thing just because it hurts your head. You are further from idiocy than anyone I've ever met. Never let anyone say that you're stupid because you're not in the usual way."

"John," Henry breathed.

"I can't let you be this necessary," John said. "We'll be in Newport in three days."

"*John.*"

John leaned in, so close that Henry could feel the warmth of his skin. "And yet I can't stop needing you."

"Then don't," Henry said. "Don't stop."

Their lips brushed. It wasn't a kiss, any more than a touch of a hand was a caress. It was just the prelude to one—a meeting of lips so glancing that it was barely even an acquaintance. John pulled back.

Henry met John's eyes, rich brown and perfect, for one swimmingly sensual moment. Then they leaned in again, and this—*this* was a kiss.

John's arm wrapped around Henry as if he could keep the entire world at bay, as if he could protect him from the end of their journey.

Lips melded, then tongues, then mouths. Henry moved to straddle John, bodies pressing together.

John was kissing him, and it was magnificent.

Throughout his life, Henry had been kissed for too many reasons—because someone was angry, because they'd faced a battle and made it out the other end alive, because Henry was *there* and he was better than nobody.

He'd never been kissed by someone who thought him *necessary*. He'd always been the frivolous one. The flighty one. He'd always been That-Idiot-Henry, and never…this. Never someone to be cherished or valued or wanted.

John kissed him as if he were air itself, and oh, how Henry wanted. He wanted so much to be the man John was kissing. He wanted to stay on this road forever. He wanted to have no destination at all. He wanted this to be his life, dust and miles and jokes and a voyage with no end.

It could never happen. They'd run out of cheese. John had a family and so did Henry.

John pulled away first. "I spent all the war thinking of nothing but coming home." He shut his eyes. "I've worried so about my sister. Now, now that homecoming is upon me…I don't want this journey to end."

It doesn't have to, Henry didn't say. But it did. It *did* have to.

"What am I going to do, John?" he asked instead.

"You're going to go back," John said soothingly, stroking his hair. "You're going to tell lies about Yorktown, and you'll be good at it. You're going to claim you struck your head and have only now recovered your memories. Your wealthy family will welcome you with open arms."

"Oh." Henry shut his eyes. "You…know about that, then."

"Mmm."

"You're not angry? I…did rather tell a pack of lies about them."

"Yes," John said in a low voice. "You did, but the lies were so obvious they don't count, sweetheart."

Sweetheart. It hurt, that endearment, coming *now*, only when everything must end.

"I have to go back," Henry said.

"I know. You don't belong here with me."

"No," Henry said. "This is awful. I inherited eighteen thousand pounds from my aunt, and if I'm dead, my father gets it all. He's terrible, John. I cannot let him have it. But how do I go back?"

"Think of this as a dream," John said. "One in which you've acted differently, but—"

Henry sat upright. "You think I'm asking how to *stop* committing felonies? No, no. You have it all wrong. That is not the question that consumes me. How do I *keep* committing treason? It's easy when it's just principles spouted on an open road. But when my mother cries, when my father shouts, when my brother calls on me and tells me that I need to think of his son's reputation—how do I go on?"

"Ah." John smiled sadly. "That, I can't tell you. But every

man's brand of treachery is his own. You've found so much of yourself. You can find this, too."

~

They ought to have fucked that night.

Henry knew that. But somehow the act itself seemed so final. Intercourse of any kind would inevitably mean *goodbye* instead of *I love you*. And Henry didn't want to say goodbye until he had to. That night, they had made a single nest of blankets.

One kiss on the lips had turned into two. John's hands had found Henry's hips; their arms had wrapped around each other.

It had only been two kisses, but the second hadn't ended. It had gone on, breath heating, until condensation gathered on the sheet of canvas they'd stretched between two trees to shield them from stray drops. The kiss had endured until water dripped onto their skin and evaporated in the heat of their want. The entire world disappeared into that kiss until there was nothing but lust and humidity. John's muscled body hard on top of him, his mouth hot against his, the ground hard beneath his hips. That kiss went on and on, until it was no different than breathing, until weariness caught them both up and they fell asleep, curled in each other's arms.

They should have fucked.

Instead, they'd awoken that morning and packed their things as if it were a day like any other day.

"Kingston?" the man at the well said at noon. "It's twenty miles distant. Just beyond, you ought to be able to find transport across the Sound to Newport. You'll be there by tomorrow afternoon with any luck."

"Excellent news," John said.

It was. Henry was not so selfish that he would count it as anything except the best news, the most perfect news. John had worried, and here they were. It was good. It was great.

It was tearing him apart.

On that last night, with Newport a three-mile walk and a boat ride away from the camp they set, they ran out of cheese.

Their eyes met over the fire as they divided the last slivers.

"It's just as well," Henry said. "It is objectively horrible cheese." It was sublime when he put it in his mouth. "Stupid reality."

"I know," John said. "I'm thinking too much of reality now. Tomorrow I find out..." Henry could almost taste his fears in that pause, the way he looked over his shoulder. He could almost imagine unknown horrors in the way John swallowed and shook his head. "Worrying won't change reality, either. Distract me, Henry."

He said it the way he said the cheese was delicious, drawing out the syllables.

"I'm no use as a distraction." Henry sighed. "When I think of what will happen after tomorrow, I come up blank, too."

John just looked at him. "That's as good a distraction as any. What *will* you do?"

"Back home..." Back home, Henry was thought a frivolous, flabby fellow. One who thought a ten-mile walk sounded like an impossibility. "Back home, comfort is its own seduction. I wouldn't even have to try, and everything would work out for me. The footmen would bow to me. Men thrice my age will take my coat and consider me a jolly master for remembering their actual names and not just calling them all Jeeves."

John's fingers touched Henry's lips, and Henry let his deepest fears come out.

"I've been pretending this whole journey. I'm a frivolous fellow. I'm afraid my ideals won't hold up to reality. How can they? The advantages I have there are…" Henry was at a loss for words, and he was so rarely without them. "…A thing." He had no better word for it. "What am I supposed to do? I can't keep telling people, no, no, don't be nice to me."

"So don't do that," John said. "There must be a thousand ways to commit felonies. You're not the sort who is meant to be rude. Don't try to be any kind of felon but the one you are."

"Mmm." Henry let the conversation lapse—something he also rarely did. He only took it up again once they'd finished dinner, cleaned up, and retreated to their blankets.

"I don't know who I am there," he said. "I know who I am here, on this road, but there? Nobody there knows…"

Me, he almost said, but he had been so many people. A frivolous child. That unthinking idiot who had taken another man's coat without knowing the man who gave it to him.

"Someone who knows the me I want to be," he finally said. "The best me. The me I can be, the me I didn't know even existed a few months ago."

"Have someone in mind?" John's thumb stroked Henry's lips once more.

Henry couldn't help himself any longer. He leaned forward and kissed John with all his pent-up desire, with every ounce of his being. He wanted, he *wanted,* to be the man who could kiss John. He wanted to be the man who thought nothing of a five-hundred-mile journey.

He wanted to be the man who, ten years from now, saw John in the morning and thought, *here is someone I can trust with my life.* Hell, he wanted to give his own life over to him.

John's arm came around his shoulder, pulling him in. Their blankets rearranged, covering each other. Their bodies came together in the darkness, as the kiss went from lips to shoulders to hips, pressing firmly into one another. It was the best kiss. The loveliest kiss. It was hard and unforgiving like the road against their feet. It was warm and gentle, like winter sunshine in the morning melting the frost on dried grass.

John pulled off Henry's undershirt—cold air touched his skin, and it pebbled—but he scarcely had a chance to shiver. The other man bent his head and touched his tongue to Henry's nipple. It was joltingly, perfectly pleasurable—that little touch, his hands spreading across Henry's chest.

Henry let out a little gasp, then a larger one. His hands spread across the other man's chest. Down his ribs. John didn't object when he pulled away long enough to get the man's smallclothes off. He bent down and tasted John's erection, licking, sucking, hollowing his mouth around the man's penis.

"Oh God." John's hands slid through his hair. "You're incredibly good at that."

How many times had Henry thought of John at night? Of giving himself over to him?

More than the miles they'd traveled together. Every time they moved, the blankets shifted. Cold air hit them in short blasts, but Henry's body was a furnace of need now.

"I want you," he said. "I want you inside me. Do you —do we—"

He never got to finish his question. He never needed to.

John turned over, fumbling in his pack. Henry knew what he was looking for. Oil, its uses all too familiar... There. He turned back, sitting on his haunches, and hauled Henry to straddle him.

John's mouth was hot on his throat. Henry leaned down and inhaled the man's scent, wrapped his arms around the man's shoulders. Their naked hips pressed together.

"God, I want you," John said and tipped his head up.

They kissed again. It was dizzying, scarcely being able to see the man. Feeling the heat of his fingers running down Henry's back. His head bowed against Henry's chest.

John's fingers followed Henry's spine, down, down. They paused. Henry could hear the clink of the glass stopper, then the cool oil, slick against John's fingers, pressing against him, opening him up. His cock twitched against the other man's abdomen.

"You like that."

"God. I do."

"Let's try a little more, then."

John's hands steadied him. Guided him onto the head of his cock. Henry exhaled, sinking down. Down. Feeling his body open up so intimately... Feeling that pressure, so right, so perfect...

"God." He caught John's face in his hands. "You're perfect, John. You're so utterly perfect."

They kissed again. They didn't stop kissing.

John's hands came to Henry's hips. They moved, awkwardly at first, learning each other, learning the rhythm of each other's thrusts. Then less awkwardly—John wrapping one arm around Henry's waist, his other hand finding Henry's aching cock. His fingers felt like encouragement, and Henry gave himself over to the feel of them. Their shoulders grew hot, then slick with sweat. Every thrust was a perfect pleasure, stoking fires that could never be banked.

Had he thought the air cold? It was hot and humid, scented with their mixing musk, the silence broken by John's gasps of pleasure.

Henry was doing this to him. Squeezing him. Riding him. He could feel the other man's muscles tense. Feel John's arm squeeze him. He felt a spurt of heat, heard John let out a groan of surprise, then thrust hard, hard inside him.

He rode out the other man's pleasure, the groans, until John was a gasping, wrung-out mess.

"Henry."

"Yes?" He could not hide his own delighted pleasure.

"How close are you?"

"Very close. I should say—"

John cut him off with a kiss. He hadn't yet withdrawn from his body. His hand closed around Henry's cock with an almost possessive groan. He pumped once, twice, his kiss hard and demanding. Henry thought of the feel of John inside him, thrusting, groaning, being laid bare...

Very close. He was very close. He was—oh God. He spilled over the edge, his wet semen painting them both. For a second, his mind could not function. There was nothing but that achingly perfect pleasure. The absolute joy of touching someone he knew so well. Someone who trusted him. Who believed in him. Someone who thought that he could be so much. It couldn't be better.

Then John kissed him. "Let me find a cloth."

It was better. There was a little water still in the canteen, and even though it was half-freezing, having someone take care of him with such tenderness, being able to return the favor... It undid Henry. More even than the sex.

They curled up in the blankets afterward. Their arms, curled around one another, spoke all the words they had not yet said.

It hadn't been goodbye. It had been everything Henry wanted—desire, affection, a promise of what they could have.

It had been a promise of an illusion, like saying the cheese was delicious. No matter how their bodies had lied, the truth was simple. Henry looked into John's eyes afterward, trying to find the right words to say.

John found them first. "You're going back."

"I'm going back." Henry shut his eyes. "You're necessary, John. I need to know that I'm necessary, too. That I can be…" He trailed off.

He didn't have to finish the sentence.

John trailed his fingers along his shoulder. "We hold these truths to be self-evident," he whispered, "that all men are created equal, that they are endowed by their Creator with certain unalienable rights, that among these are life, liberty, and the pursuit of…"

John trailed off, shutting his eyes. For one heart-stopping moment, Henry wanted to be the thing John was pursuing. He wanted to be on that list of vital necessities. He wanted to dream that he could be so important.

"Home," John said instead. "The pursuit of home."

It wasn't home in the Declaration, but happiness. Happiness was *here.* It was evident in the flutter of John's fingers down his arm, the way their bodies fit together. Happiness was laughing with a man who let their conversation ebb and flow and never called him an idiot for the rapidly turning tide of his thoughts.

Happiness was this journey, and it was coming to an end.

Henry shut his eyes and tried to imagine going back to England. Back to his family. Nothing, still.

"Go," John whispered, brushing his hair back. "Pursue."

CHAPTER NINE

They watched the sunrise together the next morning —a riot of pink and yellow and blue, tingeing gray clouds with hues that Henry could only remember seeing in a painter's palette. For a handful of minutes, the world was vermillion and gold, the unreal dream of a sleeping god.

Henry held John's hand throughout, clutching it as if it were the lowest rung on the ladder to heaven.

Then the sun rose. The clouds were gray. The dead leaves on the ground became just that—so much decaying plant matter. The dream, it appeared, was over. And because Henry was an adult and not a child, he just made himself smile. "Well. That's that. Let's be off, then?"

Their last hours together had begun.

They spoke as if it were any other day.

They had an argument on the merits of dogs and cats, and whether cats ought to have four or five toes on their feet, and if bulldogs were cute ("So ugly they're cute," Henry explained, while John insisted they were just cute without being ugly in the first place).

They spoke, and scattered farms gave rise to one village. The village tapered off but never quite seemed to end—there was always another house on the horizon, until finally the houses grew closer and closer, and the air smelled more and more of the sea.

The wind whipped around them as they approached the dock, bringing with it the scents of salt and seaweed and smoke.

"Does it smell like home?" Henry inquired.

John just shook his head. "It should, I suppose."

Henry negotiated passage and paid. John made an abortive gesture to his own deflated coin purse, but Henry ignored him, and John let him ignore him.

The waters of the Rhode Island Sound were gray and green, the waves just rough enough to keep the voyage on the pinnace interesting. Their path charted around one island, sailed between two others, desolate and craggy with shores of dark brown rock. They sailed close enough to occasionally make out yellow grasses broken by the occasional forest of tree stumps.

"What happened to the trees?" Henry asked.

The boat's captain spat. "Fucking British." It was his only comment.

"Fucking British," Henry agreed, and John shot him a smile.

It wasn't much. John's hands curled into fists on his knees. His jaw set, and no amount of Henry's cajoling conversation could soften his expression.

They landed in Newport later. The sun was shrouded by clouds, and Henry had no idea of the time. His legs felt strange on the solid wood of the quay; the world spun dizzily for a moment before his body remembered land again.

Newport had the look of a city that had seen better days.

Many better days. Weathered stone buildings with slightly less-weathered squares on their walls suggested absent metal plates, undoubtedly ripped down and stolen for the British war effort. Henry had ordered it done himself, in the early days of his commission. But if the walls of the Newport buildings were stripped bare of all possible invitation, they seemed positively friendly in comparison with the inhabitants.

Perhaps the two of them did look somewhat shabby from the road. Perhaps they were watching John. Perhaps they were gawking at the two of them together.

"Companionable bunch, aren't they?" he whispered to John as they made their way up a muddy thoroughfare.

A small smile touched John's face. "Always. It looks… different. It's been years since I was here, you know, but I spent a good decade in Newport. It's odd not to recognize anyone."

"I can pretend to know someone, if you like."

"Mmm?"

"That man there? He's a chimney sweep."

John looked over at the fellow, then back at Henry. "He's six feet tall."

Henry shrugged. "I never said he was *good* at his job."

John's swallowed cackle of mirth was precisely what he'd been hoping for.

"That woman there? She's a knight. An actual medieval knight."

"But…"

"I don't know how it happened," Henry said. "One day, she didn't die, and that's not so unusual is it? She's just continued not dying ever since."

"I do recall *her*," John said. "She sells fish." He gestured and they made their way onto an even muckier side street.

"Everyone needs a believable story to tell the masses,"

Henry said with a shrug. "Even undying medieval knights. After all that fighting, I imagine fish would be peaceful."

John just smiled again—a pretense of curved lips—and pressed his hands together.

"Now, that man—"

Before Henry had a chance to make up a story, John shook his head. "We're here." He turned, descended a few steps to a cellar door. He shut his eyes.

"John," Henry said. "It will be—" He cut off his reassurance at the flare of John's nostrils.

"Don't make up stories about my family. You don't actually know, and…" John's hands clenched. "You don't actually know."

No. He didn't. Henry bit his lip and hoped for the best. John inhaled, raised his arm, and knocked.

The silence that followed seemed interminable.

Nothing. Nothing. Then the scrape of iron on stone as a bolt was drawn, followed by the irate protest of poorly oiled hinges.

A white man, gaunt and dark-haired, stared at them from the doorway. His gaze passed over John as inconsequential and landed suspiciously on Henry behind him.

"What the *devil* do you want?" It came out on a snarl. Even from here, Henry could smell the alcohol on the man's breath.

John's fist clenched harder. He let out a pained breath, his only sign of disappointment. Someone who didn't know him wouldn't know he was upset. They wouldn't understand the set of his jaw, the angle of his ears. John was reeling.

"I'm guessing," Henry heard himself whisper, "and—I'm not sure what makes me think this—that this isn't your sister."

John cast him a repressive glance. "Good guess." For a moment, he just stared at the doorway in shock. Then he shook his head, coming back into himself. "No. Sir, I beg your pardon. I'm looking for the previous occupants of this—"

"Don't know them," the man said. "Never heard of them. No use asking." With one last suspicious glance in Henry's direction, he slammed the door.

"Well." Henry frowned. "Um. Now what?"

John inhaled. His hands were still clenched, but he raised his chin defiantly. "Now," John said, "we go to Mr. Allan."

"Mr. Allan?"

"Noah's former master." John exhaled. "He thinks well enough of me, and if—when—they departed, they would have left word with him."

"Right."

"There's no need to panic," John said, almost certainly talking to himself. "There are so many possible explanations."

"For instance—"

"No," John said. "Please don't supply them. Talk of anything else."

They made their way to the other side of the city—up a bit of a hill, from which they could see the ocean spread before them, a wide expanse of gray glitter broken by islands and dotted by French ships—before turning into a shop. The bell rang; John waited.

A rustle sounded in the back room, and a minute later, a big, burly man made his way into the front. He paused in the doorway before smiling and taking another step forward.

"John. You've lost far too much weight. You've made it back, then."

"I have." John bit his lip.

"John, I'm sorry."

"*No.*" John's face crumpled in agony.

"I tried to convince them they could stay, that we could

113

sort matters out with the constables, but things were getting bad, John. I did what I could, but…"

John's head had snapped up on the words *safe to stay*. "They're alive?"

"Why wouldn't they be? Noah left me something to give you with their direction, and I had a letter for you just two days ago. Let me find it…"

He turned to a cabinet, and John staggered, holding on to a table. "They're alive." His eyes glistened with a wet sheen. "They're alive, Henry. They're *alive*."

"Good thing you weren't worried about it."

John smiled.

"Ah!" Mr. Allan said, turning around, papers in his hand. "Here they are!"

At that moment, the door swung open behind them, letting in a burst of cold air. Henry turned.

Five men stood there. One held a rake; one a rope. Two of the others wielded pitchforks. The fifth man—empty-handed —was Mr. Suspicious, the man who had answered the door for John earlier. He stood straight; the smell of alcohol on his breath mixed with something more pungent.

"There he is!" Mr. Suspicious proclaimed, pointing an accusing finger. "Get him!"

Henry didn't think. He stepped in front of John.

This, it turned out, was a brave but entirely futile gesture. They didn't care about John.

They cared about John so little that Henry stepping closer only egged them on. One man grabbed hold of Henry's right arm; another took his left. Mr. Suspicious stalked directly in front of Henry and glared at him, his gaze raking from Henry's eyes down his torso.

"I'd never forget a man," Mr. Suspicious pronounced. "It's him. It's definitely him." So saying, Mr. Suspicious punched him in the kidneys.

Henry felt pain flash through him along with an inexplicable sense of amusement. Ha. They'd been after him anyway. How foolish of him to volunteer himself! On the one hand, he hadn't known. On the other hand—

"How do you like the weather *now?*" Mr. Suspicious bellowed.

"It's very nice," Henry said, doubling over in pain and confusion.

"What is this all about?" Mr. Allan asked.

"I would know this man anywhere!" Mr. Suspicious gestured dramatically. "He's the one what popped my knee at Valley Forge and invalided me out. He was talking of the weather and all that in the middle of battle! I could never forget."

Henry's stomach felt like a mass of bruises. That had never stopped him from talking.

"In my defense," he said, "talking about the weather is hardly an identifying characteristic. Many people do it!"

"Shut up, you."

"In fact, you started the talk of the weather," Henry went on, "so how do we know *you're* not—what am I supposed to be again?"

He got a knee in the stomach for his troubles.

"He's a British officer," Suspicious went on, "and what, I ask you, is a British officer doing behind enemy lines while his superiors supposedly negotiate their surrender? Spying. That's what I say."

"Spying on a *carpenter?*" Henry said in disbelief. "How would that—"

"He admits it! He's an enemy spy! Kill the redcoat! Kill the redcoat now!"

"I didn't admit anything!" Henry said. Which was probably good, because unfortunately just about everything Suspicious had said was true. "I'm not, I'm a—"

115

Medieval knight was the first thing that came to mind, and Henry just managed to catch those words before they came out of his mouth. *Cheesemonger* would have worked, except they'd eaten all the cheese. "I'm a—"

"Spy!" Someone bellowed. "He's a spy! Hang him!"

It was strange how the world worked. Henry had spent months wondering how to live. He hadn't wanted to die, but dying in a blaze of glory for his principles had always seemed better than any of the alternatives. So much so that every time he'd faced death on the battlefield, he'd not been afraid.

Now John was leaving and Henry had to go back and he had nothing, absolutely nothing. It was absurd that at this moment he realized that he wanted to live. He wanted it quite desperately. He wanted to figure out how to be who he was. He wanted to prove to himself, to *John,* that he was someone worthwhile. He wanted to live for years and years.

Amusing that he should learn that just as he was about to die. One man grabbed his elbow. The other took hold of the rope and gestured to the door. "The square out there," he said, "there's a—"

He never got to finish his sentence.

"He's not a spy," John interrupted in amused tones. "He's just outraged that you don't know who he is."

The men stopped. They turned to John.

"You don't know who he is? You *really* think he's a British officer?" John shook his head. "He was there when we stormed Redoubt Ten together and ended the war at Yorktown, but by all means, imagine him a spy."

"But—"

"I watched him almost die for another soldier so the redoubt could fall, but by all means, believe him a spy."

Mr. Suspicious frowned. "Who are *you*?"

"John Hunter, formerly a corporal of the Rhode Island Regiment under Captain Stephen Olney. I was at Yorktown,"

John said. "Mr. Allan here has known me a good decade—he can vouch for me. Or, if you don't believe me, write to Lieutenant Colonel Alexander Hamilton and tell him you think that Henry Latham, of all people, is a British spy."

"Colonel Hamilton?" Mr. Suspicious paused, his suspicion flickering. "Washington's aide-de-camp? He *knows* him?"

"I'm not saying this man here saved his life, but..." John trailed off. "Sometimes men look like other men. It's nobody's fault. Believe what you will. I'm just saying that I've never heard of a British officer who could recite the Declaration of Independence as if it were a prayer."

One of the men with a pitchfork let the point drop six inches. "Well, then. That's as good a test as any. Let's hear it."

Henry took a breath. One of his ribs sent a stab of lightning through him, but he could have said these words through any amount of pain. He straightened, coughed, and started. "When in the course of human events, it becomes necessary for one people to dissolve the political bands which have connected them with another..." The words came easily, smoothly, cascading one after another.

Behind the men, John gave Henry a nod. He looked down at the papers in his hand, reading through them, shaking his head.

"We hold these truths to be self-evident." Henry was speaking to John, not anyone else. He'd said these words more than once on their journey; he'd always meant them. He felt that he'd mean them for John for the rest of his life. "That all men are created equal."

After the first sentence, Mr. Suspicious waved the others down.

John folded the papers. He hefted his bag.

John was leaving. They'd agreed that they would separate here. This was no surprise. Still. Henry was stuck here reciting words written by slave owners.

"...That they are endowed by their Creator with certain unalienable rights..."

John raised his fingers, not in a salute. He touched them to his lips and met Henry's eyes. It felt like a promise of everything they couldn't have.

"That among these are life, liberty..."

"Blimey," Mr. Suspicious said beside Henry. "You really *mean* it, don't you? You're crying. You're a true patriot, aren't you? I'm terribly sorry."

Not as sorry as Henry was. John slipped out the door on *the pursuit of happiness.*

CHAPTER TEN

"John!"

Henry caught up to John fifteen minutes later, just outside the docks.

John had not actually expected Henry to come after him, but now that he had done so, he found it impossible to believe he could have been put off so easily. He'd spent five hundred miles eating terrible cheese in the hope that it would change after all.

"Henry."

They looked at each other.

"I'm leaving," John finally said. "My arm's healed, and I know where to go. I've a letter that's a mere week old that says everything's well. And the longer you wait, Henry, the harder it will be for you to return."

"I know," Henry said. "I *know*. And, John…I need to go back to my family. I want to prove I can make something of myself."

"That's nonsense. You are something. You, as yourself."

"I want to make something more. I didn't hunt you down to *argue* with you, John."

"No?" A glimmer of amusement touched John's lips. "That's a first. Why *did* you hunt me down, then?"

"To tell you…thank you." Henry swallowed. "And to beg you to write to me. I want to know…"

Everything, Henry didn't say. John didn't know how he heard it anyway.

"Thank you," Henry said. "For saving my life just now. For the entire journey. It's not that you changed my life. You made me see *I* was changing it."

John looked over at Henry. They were in broad daylight, on the docks. They couldn't embrace. They couldn't even touch. They were drawing eyes enough as it was.

"Thank you," John said, "for giving me something to believe in. Maybe a slave owner wrote those words, but they convinced people to fight for the proposition that all men were created equal." He looked around the docks, saw the suspicious looks cast in his direction. These people had tossed his family out; equals they were not. Not yet. Still… "Maybe," John said, "some day, some of them will even believe it. I cannot tell you how utterly necessary you have been to me."

"As necessary as you are to me," Henry whispered. "No matter where I go, or what I do, you and our time together will always be the foundation."

"Go." John's voice broke. He could not help it. "Henry, go now, before I do something foolish like grab hold of you and refuse to let go. *Go.*"

"Write to me," Henry said. "Write. You can reach me at my terrible father's home. It shouldn't be so hard to get a letter delivered. Just send it care of, um…the Duke of Scanshire?"

"Oh God." The roll of John's eyes was affectionate. "Of course he is a duke."

"He's definitely terrible. You'll write?"

John turned away, but not so quickly that Henry missed his reply.

"Every day," John said. "Every morning. Every night."

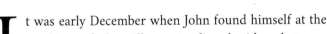

The letters from John's sister were comfort and companion on the remaining weeks of John's journey.

We were told to leave, the letter that she had left with Allan said. *Now that Noah's freed, there's talk of us becoming a burden on the charity of others. Never mind that we've done well enough for ourselves all these years. Still, we're leaving. We've met up with other freedmen, and we're heading north...*

Then, the latest letter: *We've found a space in Maine, where it can just be us, nobody else to bother us. Come join us as soon as you're able. May our love speed your feet.*

Some kind of love sped his feet—her letters, the thought of his mother in a safe space before a fire as winter came on. Imagining Henry's return to his terrible father. Henry was not here, but John imagined them having a conversation every day. It would flow over every possible topic.

He thought of Henry with every meal, with every bite of cheese that was insufficiently terrible, with every silent dinner where there was nobody about to exclaim *Squirrel! Who knew squirrel could be so delicious?*

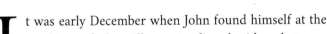

It was early December when John found himself at the outskirts of the village, standing beside what was undoubtedly a farm. The directions had taken him this far, but no signs declared names. There was, however a black woman tending the winter frames in her garden. She looked up when she saw him and smiled.

"Ahoy."

"You. You seem familiar." She took three steps toward him, squinting. "Ah, that's it. You've the look of Lizzie Hunter."

John's heart leapt in his chest. "Lizzie Hunter? Not Lizzie Allan?"

"They've taken her name. You must be that fine older brother she's always boasting about."

They were here. John inhaled and felt almost weak. "She does...go on a bit."

The woman straightened and held out a hand. "Mrs. Wexford. My husband is about, and— *Alice!*" That last came out on a bellow.

A young woman materialized from the barn, skinny and gawky. "What, Ma? I milked the cow. I *told* you already."

"Alice, this is Corporal Hunter. He's home from the war. Take him to his family, and for God's sake, let everyone know he's back. There'll be a feast tonight."

Home. John had never been to this place, but he felt himself growing roots with every step.

What was home, then, but a place where people cared about your life, your liberty, the pursuit of your happiness? Mrs. Wexford had only just met him, but she smiled at him, misty-eyed, because he belonged here and he'd come back.

He'd never been here before, but that was precisely how it felt—as if he had just come back.

This village felt like *home* in a way Newport never had. He felt that sense of belonging more and more with every step. Black children rolled a hoop down the street, laughing at each other. Every two steps they were interrupted by another person demanding an introduction. Was this Lizzie's brother, finally? They'd heard so much about him. They felt like they knew him already.

He felt as if he knew them, too, brothers and sisters in a war for independence that they had not yet stopped fighting.

"Here." Alice Wexford stopped in front of a door. Instead of knocking, though, she called out. "Mrs. Hunter! Your brother's come! Hurry!"

The door opened a scant few seconds later.

Lizzie, Lizzie. His little sister—now round with child like a prize pumpkin—her hair back, a floury apron wrapped around her—

She burst into tears and threw her arms around him. "John. You're *back*."

He hadn't let himself dream of this moment, not truly, not until now. She smelled of bread and Lizzie and *home*.

"There, there," John said. "I promised I'd come back, didn't I? You should believe me more often."

She sniffed. "You should promise less and stay home more."

He was home. Everything was perfect.

There was a feast that night, and introductions to people he'd never met but who felt like old friends nonetheless. Home. He was home.

Still, that evening, he slipped away from the impromptu gathering and wrote his first letter, because sometimes home could be two places all at once.

December, 1781

My dear Lord Henry,

My family is alive and well. They've joined a community of freedmen, and between the dozen of us, and with some help from a Quaker parish who feels the injustice done to us, we have every intent to purchase an island of our own. It is large and entirely inhospitable—hence our being able to afford it—but we have hope and determination, and so long as we make it through this first winter, all should be well...

July, 1782

My dear John,

I told you to desist. I must repeat myself. If you ever call me "Lord Henry" again, even in jest, I shall be forced to take drastic measures. It turns out that I am as good a liar as you believed. My superiors were, primed by my prior mishaps, all too willing to believe in my stupidity. After everything I'd done amiss before, my hitting my head and not remembering a thing and waking up naked in Yorktown? Apparently it was all too believable. The court-martial was nothing. They were delighted by my plan to sell my commission, as I am demonstrably less than useless as an officer.

I spent a week thereafter delighting everyone. It will never happen again.

My father was initially overjoyed by my plan to stand for election to Parliament at the next opportunity. He crowed to all and sundry that he had finally "made a man of me"—as if he were personally responsible for you Americans deciding to revolt and all that—and held a grand dinner so I could meet his friends.

In his mind, I am still not intelligent enough to develop thoughts of my own, so imagine his shock when I spoke in favor of abolition of the slave trade. Our discussion on matters of the East India Company were also helpful. I broached the concept, and someone asked, "But how will we have our cotton?"

I thought this a reasonable response: "Well, if we cannot have cotton except by means of threats, bribery, and corruption, perhaps we should not have cotton."

You would have thought I had shot a man. I published an opinion piece in the Times *the next week, entitled "Perhaps we should kill fewer people" and it has caused a scandal. It is, perhaps, not the scandal my father expected me to cause in my youth, but he has expressed absolutely no gratitude for my circumspection. There is no reasoning with him on the matter; he stands firm. Killing a man for his coin is definitely wrong, but killing giant masses of men for tea, cotton, and sugar is our particular national business and must not be scrutinized.*

Being a pariah has never been so much fun...

September, 1783

My dear Henry,

...Over winter, I intend to oversee our first major project—the creation of a handful of sloops meant for fishing. Fish can be salted and saved for the bitterest days; they can also be traded for warmer clothing, which is a necessity. But I'm hoping for something a little more frivolous. I dream of goats—there's cheese to be made, if you recall.

I have told tales of the cheese. The cheese is legendary here already, and nobody but me has ever eaten it.

The grand experiment will take longer, but my hope is that in a few years' time, we will have our first real trading vessel.

Along those lines, I finally told my mother and sister who I'd been writing to these last years. I had no choice in the matter. My mother looked at me, and there's nothing to be done when she looks like that.

Dozens of letters, she said. Is it a friend from the infantry? If so, how does he live in England?

I told them everything.

I never expected them to dislike me if I confessed the truth about my leanings—we've been through too much together not to love one another—but I did wonder if they might doubt my judgment or my character. My sister just held my hand and told me that there were enough people who thought us beneath them. She saw no point in adding to that score.

She then suggested that Patrick was single and didn't seem to have much interest in women. I had to explain that Patrick does not talk enough for my tastes...

May, 1784

My dear John,

I did not expect to win a seat in the House during the elections, but I must admit that my resounding defeat—which I have been told is an "emphatic rejection" of my "hasty and ill-conceived beliefs"—is a blow to even my inexhaustible optimism.

Even my allies tell me I must move slowly—that if we are to win hearts and minds on the abolition issue, we must hold firm on India.

Pah. I cannot stomach the thought of power won at someone else's expense. I also find that I am particularly unsuited to a career in politics. It turns out that one skill politicians must have is the ability to not say "you must be extraordinarily cruel" when someone says something that is extraordinarily cruel.

I am unsure what comes next.

I am only certain that without your correspondence, I do not know where I would be. Years may have passed since last we spoke in person, but you have always been—and will always be—the most fundamental necessity to me...

November, 1784

Number 12, Rygrove Square in London was a small house—perfect for a political eccentric like Henry who had been disowned by his father but whose mother and sisters still came around for the occasional visit.

Over the last handful of years, Henry had gradually developed a knack for political essays. His tutors would never have approved of them—he still tended to ramble, and his style was shockingly familiar instead of tendentiously formal.

But his words were fun to read, and perhaps he would change a few minds here or there.

Sometimes he dreamed of more. Sometimes he dreamed that he'd answer the milkman's knock on the door and that it would not be milk.

That was an impossible dream, one he'd learned not to indulge in too often. Henry had always been a creature of high spirits; he preferred not to lower his mood with memories of a five-hundred-mile walk.

And so it was that on a fine November morning, a knock sounded on his door.

The milkman, of course.

Henry set aside the essay he'd been writing—somehow he'd dropped a four-page aside on cricket in the middle of the thing, and it would *not* edit itself down on its own—and went to get the milk.

This morning, it was not the milk.

John stood on his doorstep. He looked—no, not older. His head was shaved completely; he stood taller than Henry remembered. He caught sight of Henry and smiled.

His smile. God, his smile. It felt like a shaft of sunlight piercing straight through his soul. It lifted his heart.

Oh, Henry thought. *Oh, this. This feeling.* He hadn't let himself remember it except in his not-so-rare lapses in judgment. He only let himself feel like this on letter-days, when he perused the pages that had come across the ocean, committing them to memory.

"Good God," John said. "You wear spectacles."

Henry yanked them away. "Only when I write—which—good God, John." His heart hammered. All the wishes he so rarely let himself feel came racing to the fore. He wanted another journey. He wanted to walk around the world with this man and never stop. "John."

John held out a block of waxed paper. "I brought you some cheese."

"Is it...?"

"No, no. It's not *the* cheese. I think some days that *that* cheese may never really have existed. But it's...something we make on the island. Someday, it might come close."

Henry took the package. "See?" He turned, gesturing John to come in. "I knew it was milk at the door and behold. Just the milk I needed."

Henry did not manage to sort out his emotions on the short walk to the pantry. Slicing bits of crumbling cheese did not help him put his thoughts in order. His feelings filled his chest like shimmering tears. He wanted, he *wanted*, he wanted still, and he didn't dare ask if this was just a visit, or...?

Their journey felt like a dream now—one where he could forget the cold and discomfort and just...remember.

Ought he to embrace John? Kiss him? Beg him never to leave? All options seemed unfair, each in their own way.

The cheese was sharp and salty with a hint of musk, a deep, rich flavor that lingered on his taste buds.

It wasn't the same cheese. It would never be the same cheese.

"It's good," he finally said.

"A bit immature," John replied with a shrug. "We've only had it twelve months now. The flavors will deepen with age."

The pause that followed lingered in awkward curiosity, like a cat that had chosen to sit atop the newspaper when one had hoped to read it.

John smiled at him. "You never used to be quiet."

"I have too many thoughts, all stampeding their way to the forefront of my mind," Henry explained. "Eventually, all but one will be trampled to death in the crush, and I shall blurt it out in triumph."

Another long silence. Their eyes met. John squared his shoulders but didn't speak.

Henry gathered his courage. "John, I—"

John spoke at precisely the same time. "Henry, I—"

They both stopped. They looked at each other.

"Well," Henry said. "This will never do. We can't trample each other, or whomever will we speak to?"

"Ah." John rubbed his hands.

"You first," Henry said, because he was a cheater.

"I've seen the newspaper," John said. "Now that you're not running for political office, I imagine you're at loose ends."

"Well, there's always next election." Henry had thought as much to himself. Next time, next time, next time... Even Henry's naturally buoyant spirits quailed at the thought of applying himself to the Herculean task of altering the British national conscience, one person at a time.

"It seems a waste of unappreciated talent. I've heard there's a position open," John said. "You might take interest in it."

"A position?"

"There's a new trading company in the process of registering," John said, "one that is determined to do things differently. You may have heard of it."

"Ah?"

"They're registering as the Lord Traders," John said.

"Cheeky bastards." Henry's heart pounded in his chest. "I like their style."

"You would."

"I must confess—I know nothing of trade. Just what I've written in my silly little essays, you know."

"Yes, well, it's not a position as a *trader* I'm offering." John looked over at him. "You see, after considerable thought, we find ourselves in need of a personable white man with a fancy accent."

"Oh." Henry swallowed. "These are...qualifications I possess."

"Someone who can say, 'My dear sir, what's holding matters up? This permit ought to have issued six months ago.'"

Henry's heart fluttered in his chest. "I am exceedingly *good* at uttering words."

"I was thinking to hire someone who could wander into a customs office and talk and talk and not *leave* until everything was settled."

"This seems suited to my talents. How do I apply?"

"The pay is, for now, quite limited. And you'd have to travel with the captain. You'd be on ships for months at a time. It's a hell of a bad deal, Henry, and the only reason you should consider taking it is because if you stay here, you're likely to lose your temper eventually and say something that will get you arrested."

"Oh, I'd say that's almost inevitable." Henry stood. "My father threatened me with it just last week, and only desisted when my mother told him to be nice."

"I haven't even come around to the worst of it." John swallowed. "I should mention that I love you."

"Oh." Henry's head spun. His heart beat, far too many times. "Oh. That's—oh. I need a little time to think this over."

John straightened and looked away. "Of course. I'll be staying here for a week. If—"

"No!" Henry took hold of his arm, turning him back. "A week would be a great deal of time. I needed...oh, two seconds. I'm already done thinking."

The stiff look on John's face softened, and he laughed. "I should have guessed."

"I had to think about the salary, not anything else. I will require a larger salary."

"Henry..."

"I inherited some money from my aunt, as you may recall. I thought...perhaps...your organization might need a little capital?" Henry swallowed. "I figured that if I was paying my own salary, I could raise it a bit. That's all."

John's eyes had widened on this at first, and then narrowed. He shook his head. "I could not ask you to do that." But he didn't pull away from Henry's grip.

"You don't have to ask." Henry shrugged. "It's already done in all but legalities. You already have my heart and my soul and my body. Why quibble about my fortune on top of those?"

John looked over at Henry. His eyes seemed dark and still, like an ocean at night. John reached out a hand, clasping Henry's fingers.

"If you need someone to say words for you," Henry said, "then I am your man."

"Henry." John's eyes shone.

"To be quite clear," Henry said, "I have never stopped being your man. Not since I started, sometime on the road from Virginia to Rhode Island."

"It's not bad, my life," John said. "My family is the best, my sister has little ones, and...I'm babbling, Henry. I miss you. In your last letter, you said I was necessary. Everything has been perfect except one thing. You're necessary—the most necessary person I've ever encountered—and you're *wasted* here."

"Oh."

"I ache, every time I get your letters." John tapped his heart. "We've tried being apart. Can we try being together?"

"How long?"

"I don't know how to measure the length of my wanting. Until the stars die and empires fall."

Henry smiled, his heart too full. "Until all men are treated as equal," he whispered. "Until everyone is allowed life, liberty, and the pursuit of…" He trailed off. *Happiness* was not enough to describe his emotion. He felt an incandescent joy, a sense that he'd finally clicked into place.

"The pursuit of home," John told him. "I told you that once, when we went our separate ways. Let me tell you it again, now."

The pursuit of *home.* That was precisely it, the thing he'd been searching for all these years on battlefields, in his father's parlor, in his political essays.

"Lizzie told me to tell you that you'd be welcome," John said. "That *we'd* be welcome. You'll like her, you know. And business will take us back here, and you can visit the members of your family who aren't terrible."

Home. Henry might have wept. Instead, he wound his hands in John's and let their fingers and their futures intertwine.

"I love you," he said again. "Please don't be disappointed when you help me pack. There's a great deal of ridiculous nothings that I'm terribly attached to and will have to bring along. I am something of a frivolous fellow."

John just smiled. "Tell me the story of everything on the voyage, then. We'll have all the time we need."

EPILOGUE

Harlem, New York, 1818

There was a clock ticking somewhere in the room, but John hadn't been able to find it yet, not without craning his neck. Which he was not about to do, not without appearing unspeakably rude. Instead it tick-tocked somewhere to his right, mocking his inability to identify it.

Mrs. Eliza Hamilton sat in a comfortable chair before them. If she thought anything of the fact that the two men before her were men, or that one was black and the other white, she said not a word.

She just poured them tea.

"It's the least I can do, when you've traveled all the way from—Maine, is it?—just to deliver a story of my Hamilton."

"Ah, it's no problem." Henry picked up his teacup and took a sip. "We've traveled everywhere; we've an office in New York now, and we were due for a visit in any event."

John looked over at Henry. Decades at sea had aged them both, but on Henry, that age gave him a gravitas that almost managed to offset the impudent spark in his eye. He sat straight; his hair was a little lighter, strands of white mixing with gold and ginger. He had smile-lines at the corner of his eyes, and his swift, irrepressible grin had left creases on his cheeks—signs that he loved, and was well loved.

At the side of the room, a pretty black woman with her hair back in a bun sat stiffly in place. She had ink and a quill and she'd schooled her face to have no expression. "You don't mind if Mercy stays and takes notes?" Mrs. Hamilton asked.

"Of course not." John gave the woman a nod. *You there, you're one of us,* he tried to convey to her silently. *I see you, not a servant.* After a moment, she nodded back.

"Well," John said. "It is…not as if we could write our story down and send it along."

"We could have done," Henry interrupted, "but it would have been terribly imprudent, and John tries to keep me to three imprudent actions per week."

"I do no such thing," John protested. "You're going to make me look the scold already, and I haven't told you no since—"

"You *never* say no, but you look it. You look at me straight on and you say—"

John couldn't help himself. "'Henry, what are you doing?'" Their words spilled out atop each other; they both stopped before they could go any further. Henry laughed. John bit his lip.

"I see," Mrs. Hamilton said slowly. "You are…friends as well as business partners." In that pause, the one just before friends, John heard everything that it would be imprudent to say aloud. Lovers. Partners. Two souls twined about each other.

In the decades they'd spent together, they had plotted and planned, grown a business from a few small lines to a half-dozen ships and three offices. When they weren't out on business, they stayed at home. They gardened. They rested. They taught children what they'd learned. What they were to one another was obvious—but their small island of freedmen had had enough of hatred and tossing people out. They had a passel of nieces and nephews. Then there were the children who were not related to them in the slightest—who were also nieces and nephews now.

"Very dear friends," Henry said. "And in a way, I suppose we owe it all to your husband's leadership at Yorktown. It all started, you see, when... No, John, you tell it."

"It all started," John said, "when Elijah Sutton was preparing to bodily toss your husband into the redoubt at Yorktown."

"Mercy," Mrs. Hamilton said to the woman in the corner, "be a dear and remind me that I absolutely must speak to Mr. Sutton."

"Of course, missus. You've already noted it once before, you know."

They continued their story—Colonel Hamilton telling John to use his name to ease his way, the cheese, the journey, the stories about how they had borrowed his name to ease their way.

They did not talk of falling in love. There was no need to admit such a thing to near strangers, and in any event, John's words, transcribed, could never capture the look in his eyes.

"After that," Henry said, "after your husband had lent his name so willingly, it only made sense to pay him back. I had some property in England, and wanted to be assured that it would not pass to my dreary brother—"

John cleared his throat.

"Did I say dreary?" Henry smiled. "I meant my *dear* brother, who has quite enough property of his own. I should hate to put him to the task of managing my funds, particularly when I have proven such an embarrassment to him. I spoke to Colonel Hamilton in New York, and he worked a bit of legal magic on our behalf."

"How lovely."

"He enjoyed my essays. We argued about government some when we were in town."

"Did he correspond with you at all?"

"Yes, we corresponded a bit. We argued about what we were building here—a nation for all the misfits who never belonged elsewhere."

Mrs. Hamilton beamed. "That sounds so much like my Hamilton."

"I brought his letters, if you'd like a copy made."

This task, too, was shuffled off to the indispensable Mercy.

"And he was most sincere in his help," John said. "He introduced me to people who have been very helpful in making our venture the success it is."

"You seem very comfortable together," Mrs. Hamilton remarked at the end. "Mercy, you're getting all this down, aren't you?"

Mercy looked over at the two men. For some reason, she looked...well, sad, maybe. Perhaps angry. Or maybe that was pity John saw aimed in their direction, for some inexplicable reason. She bowed her head over the page, though, and whatever emotion she'd shown disappeared.

"Of course, Mrs. Hamilton," she said. "I would never miss a thing."

"Well." Mrs. Hamilton smiled graciously. "Thank you both so much for the tale, and the correspondence. I suppose you have business to do...?"

"A bit," Henry said. "More like, there are people whom I'd like to see, just to have a chance to talk with them. We're growing older. It's about time for us to hand off our duties to the next generation, you know. They tend to do a better job of it."

"Sometimes they do." She sighed.

"But then," John said, "that has always been the thought, hasn't it? We make the world we can, and tell those who come next how to make it better. I suppose we'll get all the way home eventually."

AUTHOR'S NOTE

Thanks for reading *The Pursuit Of...* I hope you enjoyed it!

This story is a prequel (of sorts) to my next historical romance, *After the Wedding*—Adrian Hunter, a descendant of Lizzie and Noah Hunter, is the hero of that book.

If you want to know when that book (and the next ones I write) will be out, you can sign up for my new release e-mail list at www.courtneymilan.com, follow me on twitter at @courtneymilan, or like my Facebook page at http://face book.com/courtneymilanauthor.

The Pursuit Of... is a part of *Hamilton's Battalion*, a collaborative effort between me (Courtney Milan), Rose Lerner, and Alyssa Cole.

Rose's story is *Promised Land,* and it's about a woman who fakes her own death and pretends to be a man so she can fight for America's independence, only to have to arrest the husband she thought she left for good as a potential traitor to the cause. Alyssa's story is *That Could Be Enough,* and it's about Eliza Hamilton's maid, Mercy, who assembles the stories found in the volume—and who meets her own match in the delightful Andromeda, who has come to tell her grandfather's tale. If you liked this revolutionary romance, try them all!

ACKNOWLEDGMENTS

My gratitude must first go to my Raptors—Bree Bridges, Alisha Rai, Alyssa Cole, and Rebekah Weatherspoon—who were in the (WhatsAppChat)room where it happened when we had the initial idea for this anthology. (I won't tell you how it happened. It started out of spite. The best things usually do.) Their encouragement and help and gut-checks, from the first moment to the last, made this a better story.

Second, my thanks to Rose Lerner and Alyssa Cole, who immediately were carried away by this idea, came up with the premise for it, and delivered utter magic. You are the best partners in crime that I could possibly wish for, and in the event that I ever find myself in need of committing felonies, I will consult you first.

As always, my thanks to Lindsey Faber, Kim Runciman, and Anne Victory, for helping me deliver this story as well as I can, to my dog for his patience, my husband for...well, for nothing, which tells you that he never reads the acknowledgments, and to my vast and wonderful array of friends who are so numerous that I can't possibly list them all.

My eternal gratitude to Lin-Manuel Miranda for envisioning an America that calmly accepted me as a part of this country, while simultaneously earworming me forever.

Finally, I want to acknowledge my gratitude to you, my readers, who have been so incredibly patient with me and my slow writing. I am never as fast as other authors in the best of years, and to characterize this last year as "proceeding at a snail's pace" would be to belittle snails.

Thank you for your patience, your words of encouragement, and your kindness.

AUTHOR'S NOTE

This story touches—briefly—on the history of racism and slavery in the North, a history that is sometimes surprising to Americans who learned of slavery as a thing that existed south of the Mason-Dixon line. For those who are wondering, yes, there were enslaved people in Rhode Island at the start of the Revolutionary War, and yes, Rhode Island, after not having enough soldiers enlist, decided to open their rolls to black men—and on February 14, 1778, the Rhode Island Assembly voted that "every slave so enlisting shall, upon his passing muster before Colonel Christopher Greene, be immediately discharged from the service of his master or mistress, and be absolutely free."

This law stood in place for four months before slave owners insisted on its removal, but by that time, many enslaved men had already took steps to secure their freedom. The Rhode Island First Regiment—which was later collapsed with the Second into just the Rhode Island Regiment—came to be known as the Black Regiment because of the large number of African American soldiers who fought in it.

As for what happened afterward to John's family in

Newport, this was also an incredibly common practice. In theory, "warning out" was a practice in the New England states which was used to coerce outsiders into leaving before they could become a drain on the town's resources—usually because the town deemed them unable to care for themselves. In practice, communities warned out those whom they deemed undesirable for many reasons. African-Americans were disproportionately warned out as compared to their peers.

For those interested in learning more, I highly recommend Christy Mikel Clark-Pujara's dissertation, "Slavery, emancipation and Black freedom in Rhode Island, 1652-1842," which you can find at: http://ir.uiowa.edu/cgi/view content.cgi?article=4956&context=etd

And for those wondering how likely it was for a community of African Americans to find an island in Maine and settle there...the answer is, very likely! So likely that it's already happened. At one point, Malaga Island in Maine was settled by a mixed-race community. The inhabitants were incredibly poor, and as often happened to poor, mixed-race communities, they were eventually forced to leave. But the inevitable consequence of kicking out everyone that doesn't look like you is that those people go and find their own place.

And if you want to know what happens next to our intrepid band, well... there's always next book.

I had the idea for this novella early in 2016—what we might call a younger, more hopeful, more innocent time. At that point, my thought for what would happen in this book was something along the lines of:

1. Meet at Battle of Yorktown! Fight! Abscond!

2. ...?

3. ...?!

4. ...!!

5. HAPPY ENDING

I had some ideas, but had other projects that needed my attention first, and so I set this to the side.

I turned back to it in December of 2016. Now, it turns out that December of 2016 was a very different time than March of 2016, mostly because sometime between March of 2016 and December of 2016, November 8th happened. And...then, November 8th kept happening.

Those of you who know a little bit about my personal history know that from 2006 to 2008, I served as a law clerk—first to Alex Kozinski on the Ninth Circuit and then to Justices Sandra Day O'Connor and Anthony Kennedy on the Supreme Court. I care about this country—its legal history, its founding documents. I care about the evolution of this country in small and dorky details, like the incorporation of the Bill of Rights against the states, or the modern Commerce Clause jurisprudence, or footnote four in Carolene Products. Most importantly, I care about the Thirteenth and Fourteenth Amendments to the Constitution, amendments that came many decades after the founding of this nation, and which finally began to deliver on the most fundamental promises that were made in the Declaration of Independence—that all ~~men~~ people were created equal, and should be treated equally under the law.

It has been hard to watch the ideals (if not history) of this country come under attack—birthright citizenship, equality under the law without regard to race or religion.

This history is very personal to me. When my great-great-grandfather first came to this country, he did not bring his wife for a variety of reasons. One of them was that it was difficult for Chinese women to immigrate under the law. For two generations, my forebears lived in this country, returning to China only for brief visits to marry, visit spouses who would not come with them, and say hello to children whom they might never see again. My mother's mother is my first maternal ancestor to bear her children on US soil.

When my parents married, their marriage—between a Chinese woman and a white man—was illegal in seven states.

If I had happened to fall in love with a woman instead of a man, up until two years ago, *I* would not have been able to marry.

Progress has been good to me and mine. Regression, knowing where we have come from, is a little frightening. I found it hard on a very personal level to write a story about the founding of this nation when it felt as if I might be witnessing its end.

But there is a kind of comfort to be had in the awfulness of history—a comfort that times have been dark before and better ideals have prevailed. American ideals have always been locked in a struggle with the darkest moments of her history, but those ideals have won, and won, and won again.

It took eighty years after its ratification for the Constitution to reflect equality, and eighty years beyond that for the country to begin to acknowledge the changing Constitution. As this third set of eighty years comes to a close, I am more determined than ever to hold on to those ideals.

They have, after all, survived all this time.

OTHER BOOKS BY COURTNEY

The Turner Series

Unveiled

Unlocked

Unclaimed

Unraveled

Not in any series

A Right Honorable Gentleman

What Happened at Midnight

The Lady Always Wins

Made in the USA
Monee, IL
30 May 2023

34955602R00090